What People Are Saying About

BLUE

We live in remarkable times that call for fierce, p...
stories of great vision, especially for kids facing unprecedented changes. *Blue* offers a potent and inspiring message of truth about where we are in this world, now. And it shows us how to build bridges to the future we all know is possible ... bridges we are absolutely going to need in each and every one of our communities. Allen has built a compelling and mystical bridge to that world and our innate, awakening wisdom: our spiritual connection to Earth and the luminous web of life. Earth is calling us with urgent dreams, and *Blue* offers a path for us to answer.
Rachel Clark, science and environment writer, author of *The Blackfish Prophecy,* endorsed by Dr. Jane Goodall and Bill McKibben

***

Blue is a beautiful story of spiritual passion, danger, and transformation, culminating in a profound and surprising rebirth, as told by the gifted yet struggling Maisie-Grace. To save her dear tree friend, Blue, Maisie learns to do somersaults with her fears, grows stronger and dares to go out on a limb to express her authentic self. This is a story with powerful transformations and a joyful twist of hope and enduring trust in the continuity of Mother Nature. A child of the forest myself, this book is a treasure chest of life lessons. It strengthens your trust and connection to the natural order and the sacredness of life.
Gail McMeekin, LICSW, Author of *The 12 Secrets of Highly Creative Women,* and *The Power of Positive Choices*

Like Maisie-Grace, I grew up feeling different — dreaming with angels and having visions. "My whole life is seeing stuff without being able to say it." For anyone who feels other-than, *Blue* is a balm for heart and soul. While this is intended for middle schoolers, it's my fervent hope that this is a crossover book that reaches an adult audience, as its characters have so much to teach us all. The tree wisdom, the wisdom of children's hearts, is needed more than ever if we are to save our planet. Like Maisie-Grace, JAX, and Macon, today's children are listening to this earth's wisdom. *Blue* is a comforting guide to help us deal with the challenges we face as our earth continues to shift. "I think we live in times where we have to build our part of the bridge." With *Blue*, Allen has created a much-needed bridge for kids and adults alike as we walk into a challenging and unknown future. **Ellen Newhouse**, acupuncturist, sound healer, and author of the memoir *Nothing Ever Goes on Here*

This book changed the way I walk through the woods and think about trees — and helped me excavate my own preteen self, who went silent way back when. Imagine falling asleep curled in the roots of a huge tree as it whispers to you. Allen's writing is compelling — and she is especially good in the moments when Maisie-Grace is overwhelmed by her visions and when the old tree, Blue, speaks to her. When Allen weaves emotion, wonder, fear, and wisdom in staccato bursts and long streams of consciousness, her language allows us to inhabit Maisie-Grace's heart and feel what it is like to be psychic in a harsh and insensitive world. *Blue* is a lyrical and important book for our times, and impossible to put down. I love this book and wish I'd had it to read when I was eleven.
Madeleine Eno, book coach, editor, Human Design insights

BLUE

When hiding isn't safe anymore

To Sheila,
who passed away
and then came back to tell me this story.

BLUE

When hiding isn't safe anymore

Caroline Allen

OUR STREET
BOOKS

London, UK
Washington, DC, USA

CollectiveInk

First published by Our Street Books, 2025
Our Street Books is an imprint of Collective Ink Ltd.,
Unit 11, Shepperton House, 89 Shepperton Road, London, N1 3DF
office@collectiveinkbooks.com
www.collectiveinkbooks.com
www.Ourstreet-Books.com

For distributor details and how to order please visit the 'Ordering' section on our website.

Text copyright: Caroline Allen 2023

ISBN: 978 1 80341 692 2
978 1 80341 702 8 (ebook)
Library of Congress Control Number: 2023949023

A CIP catalogue record for this book is available from the British Library.

Design: Lapiz Digital Services

UK: Printed and bound by CPI Group (UK) Ltd, Croydon, CR0 4YY
Printed in North America by CPI GPS partners

We operate a distinctive and ethical publishing philosophy in all areas of our business, from our global network of authors to production and worldwide distribution.

Previous Titles by Caroline Allen

The Elemental Journey series (adult literary fiction) follows a mystic around the world as she comes to terms with her gift in a world rocked by climate change.

***

Earth
In Missouri, Pearl Swinton is rooted in the land of her rural ancestors, who fear her mysticism.
ISBN: 0997582405

Air
Pearl moves to Tokyo where she floats above the culture, and sees herself reflected in a homeless man she befriends.
ISBN: 0997582421

Fire
On a walk about across S.E. Asia, Pearl begins the burning of the ego that will help her own her powers.
ISBN: 0997582448

Water
In the rainy Pacific Northwest, Pearl begins a deep healing that will help her own who she truly is.
ISBN: 0997582464

Acknowledgements

My writing partner Madeleine Eno, made this process so dimensional, and I thank her from the bottom of my heart. Every two weeks for our writing exchange, we found fun places to meet—in a forest, around a firepit, in a gazebo, in my yurt. The meeting places were as interesting as the writing exchanges themselves. She read *Blue* chapter by chapter in its first raw draft, offering dimensional tips and tricks for deepening the story. Then after revising it, I threw out the first version and started over, and she was right there with me, page by page, offering her wisdom. Working with her on her middle-grade book also helped open the whimsical doors of creativity. Mad, I could not ask for a better writing partner. You are a beautiful and dear friend.

When I started writing middle-grade fiction, my friend, former independent bookstore owner Carol Santoro, piled me up with middle-grade fiction. I read book after book that she gave me, and fell back in love with that little girl I used to be who loved reading so much. Carol read an early version of *Blue* and offered support, and she continues to cheer me on. Thank you, Carol. I love how much you love books.

Colleague and friend Jerry Ryan is quadriplegic, and I hope my portrayal of JAX comes anywhere close to his wit, wisdom, and grace under fire. Thank you, Jerry, for everything you taught me.

Author and friend Ellen Newhouse is cheering me on even as I write these acknowledgments. As an early reader of *Blue*, she reminds me almost daily about why such stories are so important. Our connection to Mother Earth matters. Not being scared of the essence of who we are matters. Thank you, Ellen. Your friendship, support, and the essence of who you are matters a great deal to me.

Gail McMeekin is the author of *The 12 Secrets of Highly Creative Women*, a book that helped me become the artist and writer I am today. Highly creative girls who are empowered become highly creative women, and Gail has been part of my healing. And, on top of that, she has become a dear friend. Thank you, Gail, for being an early reader of *Blue*, and for holding the light of creativity for girls and women all over the world.

A woman with a profound connection to whales, Rachel Clark knows how important our connection to the earth is, and how we're losing that connection. She is the author of *The Blackfish Prophecy*, whose central theme is about how we dominate each other, other species, and the earth. Rachel, your excitement at reading *Blue* was just the uplift I needed. Thank you. And thank you for being a writer who is so passionate about our natural world.

This book would not have happened without my best friend, Sheila. She passed away before I even started writing this, but she guided me from the other side. Maisie-Grace is a combination of me and Sheila as 11-year-olds, full of spit, vision, and a deep mystical love for the natural world. Sheila was there the whole time guiding my hands as I wrote this story. Thank you, Sheila, for the help from the other side. I love you.

And finally, as a book coach, I work with so many writers who are writing soulful, healing books, so many writers who want to make a difference in this crumbling world. Thank you all for teaching me every day how to be real on the page, and how to have the courage to speak the truth.

Our tree became the talking tree of the fairy tale;
legends and stories nestled like birds in its branches.
Willa Cather

BLUE

Chapter 1

The child hunches over our roots in the blustery night, holding a stone in her palms. She worries it with her thumbs, stands, and raises it above her head. Opening her palms, she calls the rain to wash over it, the downpour to cleanse it.

She brings the rock to her mouth and whispers to it. That she is with us, here in the forest, in the middle of the night whispering to a stone is not new. Often at night, she has dreams. She runs down to us, finds pebbles, or bark, or fir cones, and speaks her dream-story deep into their heft.

We listen to this dream (we listen to them all), for her dreams are important. Her dreams tell the future. Her dreams prepare us for what is to come. They are not easy, a weight on such a small child. It was our idea for her to purge them into the rocks, to plant them in the earth. When we first met her seasons ago, we had not met a dreamer like her for quite some time, not since we were no more than a sapling ourself.

The child, soaked through now, dripping from red curls to bare toes, finishes the telling into the stone. She shuffles around our trunk to the back, fighting brambles and blackberry thorns, scrambling, searching. She runs her palm against our bark, letting her fingers be her eyes. Finally, she feels it, the hole at our base near one of the roots, a space no bigger than a squirrel or a large bird. Pine needles lay like a blanket on top. She palms them out of the way. Underneath are many such rocks and cones and bits of forest.

Dozens of buried dreams.

She kisses the rock and places it in with the rest. She covers them back with the needle blanket. She stands and throws her arms around us, drenched face pressed against sopping bark.

Crying, she runs from the moist forest, runs from the rock, runs from her cradled dreams.

MAISIE-GRACE

Chapter 2

My name is Maisie-Grace LaForet. If you saw me, maybe you'd think I was like some normal 8-year-old. You'd think I was weird, with crazy red hair, clothes with stripes and flowers, and boots with purple polka dots. Maybe you'd think I'm an 8-year-old clown girl.

But the problem is I'm 11. And nothing about me is very funny.

If you saw me, you would *not* know that I am the dreamer of nightmares that come true, a person who could see the future. All my life I've had dreams — about floods and forest fires, about scary fathers, sad mothers, about missing dogs and found cats. About people getting sick. About a friend's mom who dies in a car crash.

It's not much better during the day. I can read people's minds. I can see what's going to happen before it happens – even in the daylight. A gift like that makes you super popular.

Not.

Mom calls me "too sensitive."

Aunt Angel says, "Honey, that kid leaves sensitive in the dust."

The dreams happen every few months, sometimes in clusters, two or three at a time. Those are the exhausting ones. The future visions happen every day when I'm around other people. I'm OK if I'm in the forest. I'm OK if I keep as far away from people as I can possibly get.

I used to tell my mom about the dreams and the knowings, but not anymore, and I can no longer tell Aunt Angel because she'll tell Mom. I used to tell Jack, my ex-best friend, but that was before.

Maybe you think it's exciting to see the future. Maybe you think it's fun to wait for something that you know is coming that no one else sees. Maybe you think it's powerful.

It's not. It makes you jumpy. You have to pretend. People say something is one way and you see the opposite, and you have to smile and nod. You become a bobblehead dog on the dashboard of life, head wobbling with every bump in the road.

Your whole life becomes about pretending. You become a master pretender.

Chapter 3

I jump up in bed. Twister screeches a meow, leaps, and lands near the door.

No!

No!

It can't be.

It

Just

Can

Not

Be!

Another horrible dream, a nightmare, one of the worst.

I kick off the covers and run. Twister flies beside me— through the living room, out the front door, across the yard, through the forest of young trees.

Down.

Down.

Down.

It's still dark, and it goes darker and colder inside the mossy old growth. Twister shoots like orange lightning deeper into the forest. We won't see him again for a while. He runs away when I have one of my really bad dreams. He won't be back until the dream becomes reality.

"Blue!" I cry. "Blue!" I throw myself against her. The moss covering her bark is wet, and I put my face against it, tears mixing with dew. I can't catch my breath.

What is it, child?

Tears turn to sobs.

What?

I open my mouth but nothing comes. I can't tell her. I can't. I hold onto her with one hand and bend over gasping.

Find a rock, child.

I shake my head. This one is too big for any rock.

A cone? A bit of bark?

I keep shaking my head.

Is it that bad? Blue asks.

"I can't tell you."

There is nothing you can't say to us, Blue whispers, voice like the wind.

"Blue, please." I start panicking again, choking.

OK. Breathe with me, Blue says. *Come on. You know how to breathe, don't you?*

Blue says this all the time. *You know how to breathe, don't you?* Like everybody knows how to breathe. But do they? Really?

We do this breathing together all the time. I stand close to Blue's bark, breathe in oxygen, and give my carbon dioxide. It's our ritual. I stand up and put both palms on the bark, hyperventilating.

Breathe in.

Gasp. Cough. The smell is dirty and sweet.

Breathe out.

Lips close to bark. Pushing the air like blowing out birthday candles.

Breathe in.

Breathe out.

Breathe in.

Breathe out.

Calmer and calmer until I'm quiet.

Holding onto these dreams won't help anyone, child. Hiding yourself helps none of the others.

Holding on? Hiding? That's all I ever do.

My mother's voice cuts through the air. "Maisie-Grace are you down there again? Come on up now. I can't take much more of this!"

I find a big stick, turn my back so Blue won't hear. This one is too big even for Blue. I'll have to tell her at some point, but not now. Not now. I whisper the new horrible dream into it. When I try to bury it, it won't fit—it's too big. I'm trying to figure out what to do when Mom's screaming voice echoes through the dark. "Maisie-Grace, I said now!"

I have no choice but to take the stick with me.

***

Open my mouth, stick out my tongue, squish my eyes, scream a silent scream, make a blank face. Again and again.

Scream face.

Blank face.

Crazy face.

Shut face.

I take my cheeks and eyes through the motions until the blank is convincing. Mom can't know about the dream. She can't see it on my face.

When I reach the front porch, I stop and turn. Every morning I *have* to say hello to the view. We live on a huge plot of land in Oregon. Trees and clouds and grass are people, too. We think they don't feel, but they do.

The sun is rising and shooting rays through the branches. One thousand personalities stretch out for hundreds of yards— trees rolling into clouds and folding into hills. The young trees, and the old growth, and the birches, and a pond. An abandoned Christmas tree lot grown wild like a messy holiday. Wild bunnies and squirrels. A family of deer. At night, Mom and I watch the deer like TV. We've seen bobcats and mountain lions, coyotes and bears.

It's not our property, it's the landlord's. It's not the landlords, it belongs to Mother Nature. It's all so confusing. The only thing that makes sense to me is the world of the forest. The rest of the world – the quote-unquote real world – is just craziness.

Silent scream, blank face, crazy face, blank face.

15

Blank face.
Blank face.

Now I must leave the world of dreams and forests and enter the world of everything else. It takes focus. Even without the horrible dream last night, every time I wake up, I have to shift my mind from the dream world to the real world. It takes concentration. A decision. The same thing happens when I come up from the forest. I have to shift my mind from talking to trees to talking to people. It's not as easy as you might think.

I turn back toward the house. A laminated sunflower card hangs from the front door knob. This means Mom's in the shed. She must know I'm barefoot (I'm always barefoot, sometimes in the snow) because she's put out yellow shoes. I put them on, but only because of the blackberry thorns on the way to the shed.

Through the side gate to the backyard, through another gate, and across a field, the blackberry vines tug at my pajama legs like they're trying to tell me something. My insides are mush, the dream crying: *Listen to me. Listen! It's urgent!*

I was 8 when I learned to keep my mouth shut. I learned to keep my dreams shut. I had a dream to end all dreams, a nightmare so scary I could hardly breathe. I rushed to Mom and it gushed out of me like hot wind. Mom's face then, that horrified look when I told her. When the terrible thing came true two days later, when we were all slammed down by sadness, Mom wouldn't look at me. She was scared of me. She wanted to run away from me. We never spoke about it again. I lost my voice.

The field drops into a ravine. A hawk floats at eye level, playing on the wind. I watch the hawk fly and push the new dream down.

Down.
Down.
Down.

So far down that no one will ever see it on my face.

Chapter 4

The shed is a sad sight. Weeds and vines crawl up its sides, the wood is rotting and there are holes that critters get through. As I open the door, it falls in my hand, the top rotted where a hinge should be.

It always shocks me when I open the door to Mom's studio. The outside may be ugly, but the inside is like a paint factory exploded. Colors shout from every whitewashed corner, from the floor and the ceiling, too. Dozens of paintings hang from every wall. A disco ball throws stars as paper paintings flutter from a fishing line strung from the ceiling. Every surface is covered with supplies. The floor is speckled and dotted with thousands of rainbow drips.

Mom is at her easel, covered in paint. I know immediately something is wrong. Mom's a bright light, but bright lights create big shadows. Mom has big shadows.

"There you are," she says, not looking at me. "Breakfast is on your table. I want to get to the mall and get it done, so don't dawdle."

I step over Apollo who looks up and barks, and pick my way over cans of brushes and squished tubes of paint to my corner table where a bowl of muesli awaits. She's forgotten the bananas. That is definitely *not* a good sign.

I study her, at the dark circles beneath her eyes, and my heart drops. I always see it coming before she does.

"Come on, Maisie, eat up. I want to get to the mall early."

"I still haven't decided," I say.

We're going today to the mall to pick out school clothes. I've never been. To school, that is. I've always been homeschooled. If I do decide to go, I'll be entering the first year of middle school. "You told me it was my decision, whether I wanted to go or not."

"We talked about this, right? We're getting the clothes anyway," she says. She seems so tired, turns to her painting, and slashes through it with black thick paint. "Sick of this painting," she says. "Look, I told you already—you've got to have some kind of socialization with the rest of humanity." She holds the paintbrush like a sword.

"I have 'socialization'," I use air quotes, and then count on my fingers, "No. 1 with Blue, No. 2 and 3 with Apollo and Twister, and No. 4 and 5 with you and Aunt Angel." I don't add the sky or the dirt or the animals or the whole forest – she knows about Blue but we don't talk about that much anymore—because that will *not* help me win my case.

"Just go to the mall with me, will you Maisie, and not be difficult? Just once?"

When Mom registered me for school two months earlier, she told me it was my choice, but she had to register me to cover all the bases. Afterward, I overheard her talking to Aunt Angel on the phone. "I don't think being around me is good for her. She has to be able to survive in the real world...The *real* world." Silence. "Yeah, I'm taking my medication but it doesn't..." Silence. "What if I'm not around?" The last line shot through my body. Mom held her cell with hard white knuckles. I could sense her fear. Her fear joined my fear. Our fear made my stomach tie up in knots.

Back in the shed, I watch Mom and my stomach goes in knots because she's not OK now either. I finish eating as fast as I can. "OK, I'm done. I'll go get dressed. OK?" I say. If I just do what she wants, she'll be happy. Right?

She's staring darkly at her painting. She doesn't answer.

I turn to her as I head out of the shed, smile, and nod, but she doesn't see me.

***

The shopping mall is packed with parents and kids, everyone is also apparently shopping for school. This is only the third time I've been in a mall in my life. Screaming and crying and nagging and yelling and laughing – a huge ball of noise is bouncing everywhere, off floors and walls, beans me in the forehead and I can't breathe.

I drag Mom into the first store we come to.

A teenage girl comes up. "Can I help you all? I see her name tag. Suzie. "You going to a costume party?" she says to me. At first, I'm confused, then I glance around and see all the clothes are white, black, and grey.

Mom tells her we're here for school clothes, and this is the first time ever I'll be going to school. I try to catch her eye to shut her up, but she tells Suzie everything. "Do you have her style here?" she says, pointing at me.

"School!" Suzie cries. "No, no, no. Girl, no! I can't let you go to school in those. I'd never forgive myself. Aren't y'all glad you met me!"

She looks me over and guesses my size. "I think we got some petite stuff that'll fit you. "Go back to the changing room. Go on. I'll bring it right to you."

Mom and I go back and wait. Suzie comes with arms full of jeans, black leggings, grey, black and white tops, and white sneakers. Only one shirt has any color.

"These are what you'll want to be wearing," she says. "I promise. Trust me, OK? I do this all day. Every day. This is what all the girls are wearing now." She bends down to me like I'm 5, and pinches my cheek. "Y'all don't want to be standing out like a clown now, do you?"

She dumps the load in the dressing room, picks out a pair of distressed jeans, a top, sneakers. "Now, I made sure I got at least one top in your style. Go ahead. Y'all see what I mean."

I hesitate.

"Don't be shy."

Putting on the clothes is like climbing into a different person's body. The hoodie says: "Positive Vibes and High Fives" and has two high-fiving rainbow hands, and the palms come together when you zip it up. I come out of the stall.

"Oh girl, look at you." Suzie claps. "You're so tiny. How little you are! Oh, the other girls are going to be jelly of you!" She leans behind me, puts her face next to mine, and stares at me in the full-length mirror. "Big red curls, big blue eyes, y'all going to be the most popular kid at school."

My body starts buzzing. Overwhelm. I tug at the jeans. I can't breathe. I cannot breathe!

Mom sees it. I may not tell her about the dreams, but I can't hide the other stuff. She pushes me back into the stall. While I'm changing, I hear her tell Suzie, "We'll be right out."

"Oh, I need to see the other outfits, y'all..."

"It's OK. It's OK," Mom says, moving her out of the changing rooms.

When I come out in my clothes, Mom grabs the entire pile of black and gray clothes. "These will have to do. Let's get out of here."

We rush to the check stand and pay.

As we're leaving, I hear Suzie say to the other clerk. "Y'all, she was going to wear clothes like *that* to school." I turn to see her pointing at me, at my regular clothes, the striped top and polka dot leggings, and neon scarf. The other clerk giggles.

I smile.

And nod.

Chapter 5

A windstorm is rocking our car. Mom grips the steering wheel. Branches fly onto the road. Her knuckles are white, her face pushed forward, her nose like a beak. It's like the wind is losing its mind. We've always had wind storms, but nothing like this. It's like the whole planet is screaming.

By the time we drive down our bumpy gravel driveway, the winds are screeching. Mom and I screech, too, as a gust blows a limb that hits the hood of the car.

As we open the car doors, the wind takes the doors and yanks them. We fight to close them, the bags from the mall blown sideways as we run for the front door.

It gets worse as the sun goes down. I'm at my bedroom window, watching. Tall skinny trees bend until they snap. Leaves and needles spin in crazy spirals. Branches break and fly like hawks, crash and smash to the ground. Some are like spears and stab the ground, standing upright and becoming new fake trees.

All the lights go out.

"Power outage," Mom yells from the other room. She comes in with a lantern and puts it on my side table. "Oh, Maisie-Grace, for goodness sake, get away from the window."

I back off until she leaves. I turn off the lantern and put my face to the glass.

The forest dances in waves, this way and that. Rain flies sideways as thinner trees bend into arcs until their canopies touch the soil. The soundtrack is a boom and a crunch and a thud as the trees ram into each other, wood against wood. I can't see Blue from up here and pray she is OK.

Crack, boom, thump, thud.

Something is wrong with the wind. It's going too fast, too crazy, racing somewhere with nothing to stop it.

***

I wake before dawn just as it's getting light, and the storm has broken. I run outside. It's mayhem, a fallen tree blocking the driveway, a branch hanging from the roof, and evergreen needles covering everything. I run into the forest. "Blue. Blue!" I cry, climbing and scrambling over branches bigger than a person.

I'm running and someone is panting behind me. It's Apollo, who's too fat and finds it hard to run, Mom behind him.

"You can't go alone after that windstorm," Mom yells. She's in a long nightgown and house slippers, and she's hip-hopping her way over the debris. "Maisie-Grace, you slow down now!"

I hear the desperation in her voice, so I stop. I'm aching to get to Blue. Mom keeps stopping to clear the path of branches and I help her. We stand at one end of each fallen log, tug until most of it is off the path. Branch after branch.

A huge hemlock has fallen, smashing down other trees. Its massive roots are exposed, blackened, and thick and hairy. The width of the trunk on its side is taller than I am. There's no way we can move this one, we have to go around.

"So much devastation," Mom says, touching the roots of the sideways hemlock. "There are so many broken branches that we're like twelve inches off the ground as we're walking. I hate to think that Twister was outside in all of this." Apollo lumbers in circles, barking at the debris.

Aunt Angel calls Mom an "earth empath". Storms like this have a strong effect on her. Even a change in air pressure can make her weepy. She doesn't believe Angel, poopoos the idea away, even when she plunges down a dark hole, even when she stays in bed for days at a time.

I realize watching her that the darkness I felt in her in the shed – that Mom's body was predicting the storm. I've tried to talk to her about what I see. She won't hear it. She doesn't want to know.

I've *got* to get to Blue. I hike around the hemlock, and run forward, leaping over other branches.

"Maisie, wait for me," Mom cries, but I don't.

When I round the corner and see Blue is still standing, I cry out and throw myself against her.

"Look at how many branches Blue lost, Mom," I call. I walk around and count them, branches thicker than my body, with other branches growing from them, cupping upward like fingers. "Twenty-five. No, twenty-six. Twenty-six, Mom! Mom? Can she live with so few limbs?"

Mom picks her way down the messy path.

"Mom, can she live with so few branches!?" I scream.

Her face is pinched, but she says, "It'll be OK, Maisie," she says, but she's not convincing. She helps me move several of the branches away from Blue's base, hauling them to the side.

"There's no way we can clear this whole path by ourselves, and the tree across the driveway. We can't even get the car out," Mom says, standing up and rubbing her lower back. "Let me call the landlord. We're going to need a chainsaw."

My stomach lurches.

The landlord.

My dream last night. The landlord was in it. If he comes that means the dream will come true.

Not the landlord.

Not!

The!

Landlord!

"We can do it," I cry. "I'll help. We don't need the landlord. Look," I go to a branch and pull at it with all my might.

"You think you can move that tree in the driveway?" Mom asks.

"We can use the car and some chains or something."

"Ladybug," Mom says. "That's what landlords are for. I saw a piece of the shed roof fly off last night and I haven't even gone

23

to see how many paintings are ruined. I'm going to need his help to mend the roof."

I stand in front of her helpless. If I can't stop the landlord from coming, I can't stop the dream from happening.

"I'm going to find Twister," she says, walking further into the broken forest, calling "Twister, Twister." There's no use telling her not to bother, that he'll only come back when my dream comes true, which will be soon. Too soon.

I run up and throw myself against Blue. I need to tell Blue about the landlord, about how the horrible dream is coming true. I need to speak. I try to open my mouth but only tears flood out.

Was this your dream, this storm? Blue asks.

"No," I croak. "Wait, yes. A week ago, I had a dream about the windstorm. I forgot about it. Remember when it was raining? And I buried the rock?"

Yes.

"I had another dream, a worse dream."

Worse than this?

"Much worse." I feel hopeless. "If I say it, it'll come true." I know this is ridiculous. It's already coming true. But I play games with my dreams sometimes. Pretend that I have some power and control when I don't have any. That's another thing about dreamings and knowings. People think it means you have the power to change things. You don't. *I* don't. Sometimes I feel like the dreams are a stormy sea, and I'm just this tiny sailboat being tossed around.

Is it about the forest?

I nod.

If you don't say it, nothing can be done. If you don't speak, no one can help.

Something is jammed in my throat.

We ALL need to know.

"The other trees?"

All of the others.

Does Blue mean the animals, the mushrooms, the birds? I can't think.

I can see my mom coming. I move away from Blue quickly. Mom's on her cell.

"Hi, Ted. This is Sara..."

She's calling the landlord.

Chapter 6

When Mr. O'Brien's truck crunches down our gravel driveway two hours later, my heart sinks into my feet.

I sit in the corner on the porch, hugging my knees and keep watch. I don't think Mr. O'Brien can see me. He climbs over the fallen tree that's blocking the driveway and comes to the house, reaches up to the branch on the roof, which is twice his size, grabs a dangling limb, and hauls it until it falls with a crash in the yard. He yanks the limb to the side so it's out of the way. Walking back across the lawn, he climbs over the fallen tree, goes to his truck, and hauls out the chainsaw.

When he starts the chainsaw, I put my fists to my ears. The noise vibrates through my body and reminds me of my dream. He drives the arm of the saw through the tree, spitting splinters like a crazy woodchuck. The tree's too thick so he works in sections.

***

I often can see right through people. I can see who they are and who they're not. It can be confusing, the way they act versus who they are. I'm not just a "dreamer." Aunt Angel calls me a "seer". When you can see so much, people don't like it. You learn real fast how to keep your mouth shut.

Even though I was really little then, the first time I met Mr. O'Brien I saw right through him.

Mr. O'Brien doesn't really know what he's doing as a landlord. He comes over to fix something but it never gets fixed. His soul is more like a poet's—the way his thoughts and words go to softer things, how his mind doesn't go from A to B, but from A to 12 and then back to R.

"You should be a poet or a dancer," I said to him one day when he was trying and failing to fix the washing machine. I was young and dumb and used to say things like that out loud. "You'd be so happy."

He stared at me and dropped his wrench. Since then, he pretty much stays clear of me.

***

On the porch now, I watch as he finishes one side of the long trunk and goes to the other. He's cutting out a middle piece for our car to get through. The noise of the chainsaw goes on and on and on like it's never going to end. Finally, he yells, "Ho!" as the center cut of the trunk falls away. It comes to his waist, this big chunk of tree, and he shoves it with his whole body to roll it out of the way.

I run up to him.

"Maisie-Grace," he says. "I didn't see you." He moves backward holding up the chainsaw between us. Then turns and starts walking toward his truck. Fast. "Let's go help your mother fix that shed roof."

I have to jog to keep up. "Mr. O'Brien." I think if I can just talk to his poet side, if I can get him to see the forest like a poem, then my dream won't come true. I know this is ridiculous. When have I ever been able to stop a dream, but I have to try.

That thing gets caught in my throat again. "Ummm," I stumble over my words. "Umm, so, how old are the trees?"

"What?"

"The forest, do you know how old it is?"

"This property..." he stops, stretches his back, and looks behind him into the forest of new trees.

"I mean the forest down the hill, the old growth."

"It was all here when my granddad bought the land. I have no idea how old they are. For sure over a hundred fifty years. Well, the oldest ones. There's a lot of different ages."

"Can you name some of the trees for me?" I ask, pointing to the young forest. "Like what's that one?" I know they're all Doug Firs, but he doesn't need to know that.

"That's a Doug Fir."

"What about that one?" I point to another and another. "That skinny one? And that super tall one?"

"Doug fir."

"Doug fir."

"Doug fir."

"They're all Doug firs. My pop planted that whole section," he says, slowly, like I'm stupid. "For logging. You know what logging is, right?"

I turn red, nod, remember my dream, and feel like I'm going to faint.

He turns and hurries to his truck, takes a ladder off the side, and rushes around the side of the house. I run after him.

Mom is standing in the shed doorway.

"Ted, thanks for doing this," she says. She's worse. I can see it. She's smiling and pretending but I can see it.

"Let me show you the damage," she says, motioning him inside.

"What a doozy that windstorms," Mr. O'Brien says. "I've never seen anything like that." He balances the ladder against the shed wall.

"Yeah, it's getting worse," Mom says, darkly.

As we step in, he stops and gapes. "Wow!" He walks around looking at the art. "It's like I'm stepping inside your dream!"

Mom turns red, and a shadow washes over her. Sometimes shadows pass over Mom's face like clouds passing over the sun. "Why thank you, Ted." She goes to her easel. "Luckily only two paintings were damaged." She shows him the two that are waterlogged.

Mr. O'Brien goes to the back corner and surveys the hole in the roof.

"I got the roofing roll like you asked. I've already cut it into pieces," Mom says.

"Great," he says. "We can fix this, no problem." He goes outside, hauls the ladder to the side, and leans it against the outside of the shed.

"I'll come hold the ladder," Mom says.

I hover inside below the hole. I can hear Mr. O'Brien climb the ladder. His head appears through the hole above me with the blue sky behind.

They work together, Mom handing him sheets of black paper and Mr. O'Brien using a staple gun to tack each one down.

"I was going to call you in the next week, but since I'm here," he says. He glances down sideways at my mom.

I grab the back of a chair and try not to faint. I know what he's going to say. I want to interrupt but can't move.

"We're going to start logging the property, Sara. It should take a few months. We'll be taking just a few of the trees."

My dream! My dream! I want to scream, *It's not just a few. It's hundreds. I know. You're not telling the truth!*

Mom's strained voice bleeds through the shed wall. "You didn't say anything about logging when we moved in."

"Your lease covers a couple of acres near the house." He hits the staple gun hard against the roof like he's mad. "We let you roam the property, but you know the woods aren't on the lease."

I'm falling down a hole and can barely hear. I stare up at Mr. O'Brien's head. More of the patches have gone up and already half his face is gone.

"There's this log cabin company in Idaho that's buying up the taller Doug firs," he says. "They aren't going to be chopped up, but used whole to make cabins."

Mom is crying, a soft sound.

"Now Sara," Mr. O'Brien says. "This isn't your business. This is my business. With this storm, and all the wildfires...we gotta get them out of there while they're still worth something. These trees are our bread and butter."

I see tears coming into Mr. O'Brien's eyes, well the one eye I can still see. Mom keeps crying and he grows angry again. "Look, this is a logging town. You know how this works. You know what you were getting into when you rented this house!" He puts on another patch and hits it hard. Almost all of his face is gone now, except his right ear.

"When?" I scream, louder than I mean to.

"Oh, Maisie-Grace," Mom says through the wall.

"I need to know when!"

"Sometime in the next month, but it'll take a while, so you'd better prepare yourselves. It's going to be noisy and it may last a while."

I want to run out and push the ladder and hurt him like he wants to hurt the forest.

What can I do? What can I do? My mind is spinning. I feel something against my ankles. I look down.

Twister, orange fur matted, wet, and smelly.

I pick him up and bury my face deep in his filthy neck.

Chapter 7

It's like the forest is a mall and price tags are dangling from the branches.

"They're going to log the forest!" I cry to Blue.

My shaking hands push the story into her bark. I tell her what I dreamed. What the landlord said. What the loggers will do. I push the story through my palms like a prayer.

The words move like liquid through Blue's roots. Vowels and consonants drop on the caps of mushrooms growing around gnarly roots. Subject, verb, object absorb into the dirt, travel underground, wash toward the other trees. I feel the whole forest buzzing with the news.

When? When is this going to happen, child?

I bite my lower lip. "In the next month or three weeks or two weeks. I don't know!"

I hate that answer. Does it mean tomorrow? Next week? When?

Talk to the others.

"They already know," I cry. "I felt it." I feel I'm growing roots too, that the story is traveling through my roots too. I feel like a tree.

We didn't say tell the others. We want you to talk to the others. All of the others.

I don't know what Blue means. She talks in riddles. Still, I walk into the forest, sliding on wet roots, dangling moss brushing my cheek. I touch each tree. I choke out my sadness, my voice a whisper.

"I don't know which trees will be cut down," I tell them.

"I'm sorry," I say.

"I'm not sure when."

The trees sway and moan, a low hum. I cock my head to hear, and it's really there, the voices. It's been such a long time since

I could hear the whole forest. The humming becomes singing. The trees become personalities. I can see them as individuals. Trees as people. It's like their voices are coming through a fog, a fog in my mind.

I can't do it.

I can't do it.

I can be friends with Blue, but I just can't take on an entire forest. I can't.

I run out, past Blue, into the light, up the hill.

Child, please. Please! Blue cries.

"I can't, Blue," I cry. "Blue, I just can't."

Chapter 8

I'm under the covers with Twister when I hear a tap on the door. Mom comes in and sits on the bed. She holds my ankle through the blankets. She's upset, too. First the wind storm and now this. She's never believed in owning land. She doesn't believe anyone has the right to own a tree. It's something she told me once. "Spirit gives us land and trees and animals. They don't *belong* to anyone."

It's not like the forest is something in the background to us. It's family. To even think of living without them is like living without a house or a mom.

Mom crawls into bed. Her singing is soft. "A-ma-zing Grace, how sweet the sound..." She has a voice like tiny bells. The last time I remember her singing that to me was when we first moved to this house, when we finally got away from my dad. I haven't seen him since. He has his own crazy wind.

The song is how I got my name.

"I'm sorry, Ladybug," she says.

I feel something welling up, something big and important, like for a second my throat isn't blocked. The words come out of my mouth in a rush.

"Let's save Blue, Mom." It's like I've been thinking this the whole time since I had the dream, thinking it and not realizing I'm thinking it. Of course, we can save Blue. "Let's get Mr. O'Brien to leave Blue. I bet he will."

"OK. OK," she says, excited now too. "Let me talk to him."

"We could tie a ribbon around her and ask the loggers to leave her," I say.

"I'm sure he'll agree," she says.

"We'll tell him how much we love Blue, and get her a ribbon, and she'll be fine. She'll be fine," I say.

She'll be fine.

She'll be fine.

She'll be fine.

Mom gets into bed and curls beside me. I feel myself falling but jerk myself awake.

I don't want to sleep.

I don't want to dream.

Chapter 9

In the morning when I tell Blue the plan about the ribbon, she says: *What about the others?*

"Blue, how can I save you all?"

The others, the others, Blue keeps saying. I want to talk about going to school. I have to decide today, and I need advice.

The others. The others, Blue won't stop. I figure Blue is upset and can't make sense today. Neither can I. Nothing makes *any* sense.

As I walk back up to the house, I see Aunt Angel's car. I run and burst through the front door. She's sitting at the dining table.

"Kid!" she bellows. I run and throw myself into her arm.

She's big and round and tall. She wears crazy dresses with bright flowers. She smells like peaches. She smooches my hair, a thousand butterfly kisses. She's not really my aunt. She's Mom's best friend. They work at the same bookstore. Angel reads tarot cards in the back room.

Angel launches into stories about her tarot clients. She doesn't bring up logging or school and I'm sure Mom's been talking her ear off about both, and I could hug her for not saying anything about any of it.

"This woman comes to me and she's got this lottery ticket in her hand." Angel holds up her napkin like it's a piece of paper. "She says, 'I gotta know if this lottery ticket is a winner!' She plops 65 *dollars* on the table. She's paying me 65 *dollars* to tell her if she's won the lottery!" Angel spits out an olive as she's laughing. "I'm like, 'Isn't the lottery drawing tonight?'"

She's shaking her head and guffawing, and Mom and I are giggling, and it feels good to laugh.

She tells us about a woman named Lucy who keeps calling to speak with her dead cat. We've heard about her before. Lucy has had dozens of readings with Aunt Angel over that cat.

"So, I pull the cards on Melvin. He's a talker. Melvin's like, 'Honey, it's been five years, get over me already'."

Aunt Angel is popping chips in her mouth like popcorn. "I'm channeling Melvin. He's chattering away. Melvin is telling me to tell Lucy to go to the shelter that Friday because a white kitten named Aphrodite is coming in. 'Adopt Aphrodite!' I mean Melvin couldn't be more clear.

"But Lucy is just weeping. She's been sobbing over Melvin for *five years*. Sometimes she pays me for a *whole hour* and cries the *whole time*. Finally, Melvin says, 'Sister, I'm not gonna be happy in the afterlife unless you adopt Aphrodite.' She's still crying. Melvin is like 'Oh, dear lord, I wasn't that great of a cat! I was ugly and mean and used to scratch everybody!'

"So, days later Lucy calls and tells me it happened just like dead Melvin said. She went to the shelter and there was a white kitten who'd just come in and they were still naming her and they were leaning toward Aphrodite, and how she'd cried and said, 'The kitten is mine. Mine!'"

Aunt Angel is now wolfing down chips and dip, crumbs piling in her lap. She holds up a finger while she chews. From behind her hand she says, "She called me this morning because she wants another reading. She wants Aphrodite to talk to her. She wants to know if Aphrodite loves her as much as she loves Aphrodite! She was *sobbing*."

We all laugh. Angel has read Twister's mind for us, and Apollo's – we all believe animals can talk. We know Angel can hear them. It's just the way she tells the story makes everything she does seem funny; everything seems silly and just fine.

"So, kid, what's the moral of these stories? Just because you *can* talk to the other side, doesn't mean you want to live there all the time. You also gotta live in the real world!"

I stare up at her. She's looking at me. It's like she's reading my mind.

Mom's phone rings.

"I'm going to run to the girlie's room," Angel says, and a wave of peach scent wrapped in chips and almond dip wafts over me as she gets up.

Mom says, "Oh, Ted, thanks for calling back."

I tense. I know it's about Blue, about saving Blue, about tying a ribbon around her and protecting her from the chainsaws. Mom excuses herself and goes back to her bedroom.

I stand at her door and listen.

At first, he must say no. Mom asks if there's any way, and then she goes quiet. Quieter than just listening. And I think they've hung up. I think that all is lost. That's the weirdest thing about being able to talk to trees and animals. Everybody else thinks they're things and property so they don't care, and you're standing at a door listening because it's life or death, because it's the death of your best friend.

I hear Mom speak.

"How much?"

There's quiet, too much quiet.

"OK, then, we'd like to buy Blue."

Chapter 10

I'm frozen against Mom's bedroom door when I feel a hand on my shoulder.

"Kid, it'll be OK," Angel says, "Come on. Come sit." I follow her blindly. Angel doesn't have to hear what's going on to know something is going on. She leads me back to the dining room.

I walk like a zombie to the table. Mom doesn't have much money, but that's not the only thing bothering me about her buying Blue. She doesn't believe in buying nature. I don't know what it means that now she's buying Blue. I don't know if some line has been crossed that can't be uncrossed.

And something else is bothering me. I get a strong vision of Blue, standing there all by herself, the rest of the forest floor covered in stumps. And for the first time, I wonder and worry – Can Blue live completely by herself? Does she need the others? Is it better if she dies along with them?

Angel is moving the small plates from the table to the counter.

"It's time for a good old-fashioned tarot reading," she says.

She grabs the carpet bag she always carries, and pulls out a candle, matches, incense, crystals, and a round cloth. Angel is like Mary Poppins with that bag. She's read my cards before, but Mom doesn't really like it. She says I'm not old enough.

I want to ask her everything, about the logging and about school and about purchasing trees, but Mom's there and I can't. Angel places everything in the middle of the table and lights the incense. The incense smells musky and sweet.

Mom comes in.

"Angel?"

Angel puts up her hands. "Come on Sara. She's old enough for a reading."

"Keep it light. I mean it."

I try to catch Mom's eye to ask her about buying Blue, about the money, about the rest of the forest, but she won't look at me.

Angel mixes the tarot cards and holds them to her face, whispering prayers into them. It reminds me of me telling my dreams to rocks.

"OK, kid. We know you've got some big things going on. Let's start with a general reading, OK?"

She fans the cards out. "You know the drill. Pick three. Turn them right side up." Angel spreads her arms wide and makes circles with her thumbs and forefingers. Her energy grows big, fills up the kitchen, the whole house, and busts through the ceiling until she feels as big as Blue.

"Light, I said," Mom warns.

Running my palm above the cards, I come to the middle of the spread and stop. "I feel it here." I pick a card and hand it to Angel.

"Wowzah!" Angel screams, her voice booming. Twister runs and Apollo barks. "You don't do things by half!"

"Angel is this light?" Mom yells over her.

"Sorry, was I screaming?" She winks at me. She changes to a dramatic whisper.

"Baby girl," she says leaning toward me. "The first card you picked represents Change. It's not just that you're going through change, which we all know you are! It's also saying something bigger. Like you're a change agent. Do you know what that means?"

"Yes," I say but I don't.

"A change agent is someone who changes the world! She's also someone who creates change. Are you picking up what I'm putting down?"

I nod.

"Next card, kiddo."

I do the same, run my hands over until I feel something, and hand Angel another card.

She takes it, looks at it, smiles big, flips it around, and holds it up to my face. On it is a massive tree. It's nothing like Blue. Blue is a Douglas Fir and her trunk goes dozens of feet up until you come to any branches. She has needles and not leaves. This is more like an oak tree with normal branches and normal leaves.

"You are the keeper of the forest," Angel says.

Keeper of the forest – the phrase dances up and wings into me, into my heart. *Keeper of the forest!* I feel like a superhero.

Angel studies the card, and it's as if the card is speaking to her. "They're saying it's a big responsibility being the keeper of the forest. A big responsibility. Not everyone can feel and see the forest like you can, so don't expect that of them. It's a gift given to you...and to others, and throughout your life you'll meet these others. Sometimes, though, you may get tired being Keeper of the Forest in this world where a lot of people don't care. You have to tell the trees so you can have a break, you have to say, 'Today, I'm here to just enjoy a walk in the woods. Today I'm not keeper of the forest.'"

She puts the card to her ear. "Anything more?" she asks.

"Branch out! Branch out! This little voice keeps saying that. 'Branch out!'" She flings out her arms and starts singing like she's an opera singer. "Braaaaaaaaanch Ooooout."

Mom comes over with a plate of cookies. "Cookie, Angel?" She puts a cookie in Angel's open opera mouth.

"Oh, they'll try to shut you up," Angel says, talking with her mouth full, grabbing another cookie before Mom leaves. "But change agents speak no matter what."

I pick the final card. "Fight!" Angel nearly yells when I turn it over. "Fight! You have the right to fight for the world you want to live in!"

I start crying. I can't fight. I don't know how to fight. I'm already so tired. Everybody already thinks I'm so weird.

I can't stop crying. I don't want Mom to see this but I cannot stop.

"Angel, I *told* you it was too much."

"Much much," Angel says, that's the phrase she's used with me my whole life when I get overwhelmed. She twirls one of my red curls around her finger and kisses my sweaty forehead. "Much much," she says.

Mom swoops in and gathers the tarot and puts the deck into Angel's carpet bag. "Enough."

Mom starts petting my hair, but I shrug her off. I'm mad at her and I don't know why.

"How, Aunt Angel? How do I fight?" I try to scream, but my throat closes and it comes out a whisper.

Chapter 11

Mom takes Angel by the arm and pulls her out of her chair. "Maisie we're going to the art studio. Could you clear the dishes?" She drags Angel out the back door.

I give them a few minutes, sneak out, and follow them.

The door of the shed is hanging open. I hide to the side. They're talking about me. I guess I'm not hiding my dreams so well because Mom's talking about them, but she's too far from the door and I can't really hear her. Angel is near enough and her voice is booming.

"... I don't know, the kid's got the gift, Sara. What are you gonna do about a kid born with the gift? Hope it'll just go away? Protecting her obviously isn't working. She's way too smart and way too psychic," Angel says.

"Don't use that word!" Mom says.

"Which word? I used several."

"Psychic."

"Well, I didn't know you hated psychics. I'll make a note of that. Maybe I should just go."

"I don't hate psychics," Mom says. Angel snorts. "I don't. I'm just so scared for her...I want her to have some kind of normal life." She says something about sensitivity and other stuff I can't hear. She has a soft voice, and Angel's is like a bellowing wind.

"You going to try and stop her dreaming, Sarah? Come on. This reminds me of how your mom treated you, how she didn't want you to be an artist. How she still judges your lifestyle. Aren't you doing the same thing to Maisie?" Angel asks.

"That's *not* what I'm doing. It's not! A kid shouldn't be having such dreams, Angel," Mom cries. "It's too much!"

They start talking about the "big dream" – that dream I had at 8 years old that scared my mom and shut me up *forever*.

The dream about JAX and her mom that changed everything, the dream I do everything in my power to forget, but it still plays over and over in my mind. I remember it like it was yesterday.

JAX and her mom are driving, the dream dark around the edges so I know it's one of those that comes true. A truck veers toward them. Mrs. Watanabe jerks the wheel, and the next part is a screeching, and twisting, and tumbling, fast but in slow motion. The car skids, and flies and tumbles down a ravine, rolling and rolling. I see JAX trapped in the passenger seat. I see Mrs. Watanabe's spirit leaving her body. I watch her soul travel above the car and turn into a cloud. In the dream, her soul feels beautiful.

I ran and told Mom afterward. I was used to telling her my dreams then. As she listened, the dark cloud blew in and covered her face. She recoiled from me. She left me standing and went to her room.

When it didn't happen in the next few hours, I could see she was relieved. She didn't get that it was going to happen. It just hadn't happened yet. I didn't tell JAX. Why didn't I? I always tell myself it was because I was little then, too young to understand, but I told her all my dreams then. I could've tried to call her. Was there a way to stop the dream from happening? I didn't think so. I still don't think so. But maybe, if I'd called her...I ask myself this every day, *Why didn't I tell JAX?*

When the phone in the kitchen rang that night, I knew. I knew everything was about to fall down the rabbit hole. Mom hung up and stared at me. I'll never forget her eyes. The fear, the anger. I'd never seen her so angry. She locked herself in her room. It was like she didn't want to be in the room with me, like she didn't want to be near me.

That was the moment the Great Pretender was born.

***

Now at the shed, Mom has come nearer the door and I can hear her clearly. "I don't want her life to be full of all this kind of anxiety. She saw Mrs. Watanabe die, Angel! I don't want it!"

"How can you stop it?"

"I don't know. It's not good. It's just not good."

"Kids these days are seeing a lot more than we ever did, Sara. Kids don't even have to be psychic to see things the likes of which we never had to handle," Angel says.

Mom says something but she's moved to the back of the shed and I can't hear.

"Look, I've been reading a lot of tarot for clients with sensitive kids," Angel says. "The message I'm receiving is that a whole new generation of empaths are coming in and they have a purpose in this screwed up world. Their high sensitivity is going to force change. But it's hard as hell. They have to figure out how to be a bridge in a world that's not sensitive or aware at all."

Mom must've done or said something because Angel bellows, "Her dreams are important, Sara!" Angel pauses and says, "If I were you, I'd focus on helping her figure out what to do with the gift."

This time I hear my mom clearly. "I don't think she should go to school. The rest of the world is horrible!" she says. "Violence! And twisted up thinking. I don't want her near that! She's not going to school! What was I thinking?" Mom is getting twisted up. First, she wants me to go to school, then she doesn't want me to go to school.

"You've kept her locked up for 11 years, Sara! I think your reasons for registering her for school were good ones. She needs to see what the rest of the world is like. Maybe she has something to offer. Maybe her going to school can help the world. It's important that she gets out there and meets the others."

The last two words send a jolt through me. *The others. The others.* Blue's voice mixes with Angel's. *The others. You have to tell the others.*

"I'm going to school!" I scream now from outside the shed.

"Maisie-Grace?" Mom cries. She and Angel rush to the open door.

"I'm going to school!" I yell again. "I want to go. I'm going! It's my choice."

BLUE

Chapter 12

When we first met the child, she was not OK. Her mother was not OK. They were bruised in spirit and tired in soul, and they'd come to us to heal. We saw all of this immediately. The child was little. The mother threw a ball to a puppy they call Apollo. Even then, the animal would not run.

Well, we haven't met anyone quite like you here in a very long time, we said to the child.

"What?" She looked around. "Did you hear that, Mom?"

"Hear what?" Her mother cocked her head to listen.

Will you come speak to us?

The child glanced this way and that. She walked forward.

Back here.

She turned and came toward us.

Nice to meet you.

She put her small fingers on our trunk. "Your bark is moving," she whispered, "like it's alive."

It's because you can see us. We laughed.

She looked into the dark forest, the moss hanging like hair. "It's like the whole forest is singing or humming. I didn't hear that before."

It's because, child, when you can hear one of us, you can hear all of us.

She threw her face back and stared upward. "You're so tall. I can't even see all your branches up there."

Yes, very tall and very old. Can you see how my bark has stretched? Can you see the gashes?

She put her palm over a furrow. "It hurts?"

Sometimes.

She leaned against us, her chin cocked upward against our bark. "Oh, from way up there I bet you can see everything."

We told her about the flying squirrels and the baby birds in nests, about the way the tops of some of the evergreens flop sideways.

"Maisie-Grace," her mother said, laughing. "Are you talking to that tree? What's she saying?"

"She's just saying hello."

Her mother backed up and studied the top of the old tree. "I'd like to paint her. What do you think? Doesn't she look blue to you, Ladybug? Prussian blue, I think."

That's how we got our name.

The child came every day, then, with her mother and the dog, and later to show us a newborn kitten. She came to read books with us, eat with us, and count our mushrooms and pinecones. She sang, danced, and breathed with us. She collected bits of us that fell to the forest floor. When she started dreaming, when the knowing became too much, we asked her to tell us the dreams, so we could take them and mulch them. Then when we knew that someday she'd want the dreams back, we suggested pouring the dream into a rock or cone and burying it with us.

We are what humans call a Douglas Fir. Once, Maisie-Grace said, "It's so funny you're named Douglas because you're a girl, but you have a boy's name."

No, we said. *We're not a girl or a boy. We're a Blue.*

Oh, how the child loves us, the mud, the rotting. She roams and touches—spongy moss, saplings sprouting from logs, miniature gardens growing from stumps. She'd say to us often, "Oh it's like living in a fairy tale."

Her knowledge of us is not in her mind, but in her senses, in the smells and the textures. Flesh of our flesh.

The forest is in her fingers, running along rutted bark, playing with the stringy moss, her palm on bleached snags, tracing her fingertips along the patterns left by bark beetles.

Once she said to us, "In the fog, there are ghosts. Do you see them, Blue? They're not scary. Ghost hawks and ghost owls. They're puffs of white that take shape and float away." Oh yes, we were familiar with the ghost trees and the ghost animals, how they emerged and merged.

How she reaches down and picks up pieces of us, pinecones or pebbles or sticks, and puts them in her pockets, how she takes us home with her.

***

Today, the child is tying scarves around our bole. Today, the wind brings the story of fire from forests far away. We feel the smoke high up in our needles and down below, sinking into the soil. The child smells it too, and she ties the scarves tighter and tighter. "To keep you safe," she says, but we can tell she is nervous.

She tells us all about going to school. And we are glad. We are relieved. We have things we want the child to pass on, things that require she make her way into the world.

We want to say some things, we tell the child.

"OK?" she answers, making a bow at the end of the scarves. "I'm listening."

We want to say important things. We want you to really hear us, to remember. We want you to share it. With the others.

The child sits next to a village of mushrooms and studies a pine cone. Her head down, she says, "You can tell me, I'll listen. But I can't promise anything else."

We must. You must. Will you write it? Please?

"I don't have anything to write on," she says. We wait. She plays. We wait more.

Child!

"OK, I'll go get my notebook," she says.

She runs away and comes back.

We draw nutrients from the roots, sucking them up our bole, pull sugar down from needles high on the canopy. Pulling all of the energy to us so that we might speak, we might be heard.

Ready?

She nods. "I guess."

We will try to speak to you with words but it is not with words that we live. You know this. We commune in something other than words, in rain and wind, in nest and burrow.

Are you writing it down?

"Go slower."

We slow.

We'd rather not speak at all! We'd rather just "be", but today the wind brings songs of flames from other forests. We would rather just be, but that is no longer possible. We must speak so humans can hear.

"I understand not wanting to speak," the child says.

This is the first lesson then.

The child is stuffing pinecones in her pocket, building a pile of sticks in front of her.

Are you listening? Are you paying attention? Are you writing it down?

She takes up her pencil.

We use the word "we". People use the word "I". We want you to understand the word "we".

The child is slow in writing.

People used to know our language. People used to know the "we" of the forest, and the "we" of people, how we're all one. They have forgotten the mother tongue inside their own noise.

The child curls into the nook of our roots with her journal as if she is cradling it. She is a good one, this child. She is one of the few who can still hear us. We know it's not easy for her among the others.

Did you know that a long time ago, when forests covered the land, there was no edge? Imagine a blanket of us covering the earth. We once lived "amidst" and now we live on the edges. When we were many, we all lived within, cocooned inside each other. Now, so many of us have been taken that we are all on the edge. When we are on an edge, humans are also on an edge.

We are you.

You are we.

We are we.

We stop for a while and watch the child's hand move across the page. We feel the wind in our branches, and the wind in the child's arm as she writes, and we know it is the magical wind.

We are not just bark and branches. We are hawks and squirrels, insects, and woodpeckers. We are birds. We are roots and mushrooms and worms. We are an orchestra with many instruments, singing night songs. People see this one tree or that one tree or that shrub or that plant and think we are all separate beings. But we're not! We're not separate!"

"Yes, yes," the child whispers, in a trance now.

We say nothing for a while. Even after she's stopped writing, we sit in stillness, listening to the tweet, and caw, and pitter pat of the forest. Then we continue.

We are all together, we're all tumbling and crumbling into each other and over each other. We are not separate. We cannot be. We are the soil, the sun, the rain — we are a sum of many parts. We are greater than the sum of all parts.

We live through many of your generations, high above in our own worlds. Maybe you think we live to "watch over you". But you are we. We watch over we.

The moss growing on our bark mixes with the child's hair.

We are you.

You are we.

The child rests her whole body against us. She is no longer writing. She's hearing beyond words now.

You see us, child. That is all. You are more "us" than "them". You are a sapling. A few are born now like you, open ones who can hear. This brings us great relief. Child, are you awake?

"No," she says, "I am sleeping inside of you now."

We live in slow motion. Can humans learn to be slow? You zip and rip and flip, so fast. Slow is clarity, is safety.

Some like you come to us "not knowing", come to us with a clear mind. Most, though, come with sword-brains and intentions. You come with openness and soul-nothingness.

They used to know us.

They used to know.

We stay for a while without words, the child sponge and sap, needle, and root inside of us. We live where no words are needed.

Child, there is one more thing.

"Yes?" she says, stretching, waking up.

You must share all of this with the others.

The girl shakes her head in tiny movements. She leans forward and fills her pockets with twigs with more needles, rocks, cones, dirt until they're almost bursting.

"I can't. I can't," she whispers.

She stands up, starts moving backward, leaving our world now for the world of the humans.

Child, listen. It's not just about us. It's about all of us. Tell them what I have told you.

"I can't." She turns and runs. "I can't," she cries. "I'm sorry I just can't!"

MAISE-GRACE

Chapter 13

Aunt Angel and I are in the shed. I don't like being here. I need to be watching for the loggers. Every day, I pace and wait. Every noise from the road makes me jump. I pace the driveway, the front yard, the living room. I stand at the front window with binoculars for hours, wanting to see the faces as they drive in, wanting to see what kind of people would cut a whole forest down. Mom is in bed. I saw it coming, and it came. It's the windstorm, the landlord, and the logging...it's the smell of wildfire smoke, buying Blue...it's all the above—Mom won't be coming out of that dark room for a long time.

"Hey, pay attention, Kid." Aunt Angel says. I'm sitting at Mom's art table, and Aunt Angel is holding up my favorite doll. She flops the doll at me. "I asked you a question."

"What?"

"Who is this?" She flops the doll at me again. It was my favorite when I was 5, with red ringlet hair like mine and her own dresser drawer full of tie-dyed clothes, a hippie rag doll. Mom had to resew her legs like a hundred times because Apollo thought she was a chew toy.

"Sweet Pea," I say.

"Nope. Today, she's not Sweet Pea. Today she's *you*."

This is my official "school bootcamp", as Angel calls it. Apparently, I need a boot camp to get ready to go to school.

Angel holds up a yellow block in her left hand, with Sweet Pea in her right. "What's this?" she asks.

"A block?" I don't understand this game. Why is she treating me like a slow infant?

"No, this is the school bus." She puts the doll and the bus together. "This is you, getting on the school bus."

I roll my eyes. "I'm not stupid! Ugh."

Angel flounces toward me and puts a long red nail in my face. "Now you listen to me, kid, or you're never going to make it. This world is nothing like you've ever experienced. I'm going to do my best to get you ready, but you better be clear. This is a battle you're going into, you alone, and you alone are going to have to fight it."

I face plant on the table.

Aunt Angel lifts my face. "I know how much you see things. I'm not here to teach you anything at all about how to 'see'. You already do that."

I cover my face with my hands. It's too much. I can't do this.

Angel pries my fingers away. "Kid, you asked for this, right? You want this. When you ask, and the universe answers, you gotta pay attention. That's really all the universe is asking, for your attention!"

I sigh. Sit up straight.

"Good. Perfecto," she says, rushing to Mom's easel. She's clipped a big pad of paper there and flips through until she finds a rough drawing of a road with houses, buildings, and trees. A long arrow travels from a small house with "home" written inside it and a big building at the end with the word "school".

She puts the doll on the block and starts at the small house. "You're comfortable when you're at home, right?" She moves the doll and block over the line that's a road. "So, now you have to create an *emotional* bridge to the other place. From being alone...cross the bridge...to the front lines. See? You need to bus to make the transition."

I get what she's saying. When I come up to the house from the forest, I have to shift my mind and get ready for the "house world", with its own language and its own ways, like I'm visiting a foreign country. School is now another foreign country. But I've had years to figure out the transition from the forest to my house. And right now, I only have a few days.

Aunt Angel takes her large "Mary Poppins" bag and lugs it onto the table. She digs around and comes out with a massive old red hardback book and plops it on the table. A plume of dust wafts up from it. "I brought you two books, kid. One from the ancestors and one that's modern. Couldn't figure out which one would be better."

She digs around some more and comes up with another hardback. This one is brand new and shiny white.

I touch the red one, the lettering so faded, I almost have to read it with my fingers like Braille. "The Alchemy of the Sacred" it reads. I'm scared of it. I open a page tentatively and see hand-drawn pictures of chamomile and rose hips, and shut it quickly. It pulses with so much energy.

The other one's title is clear: "1001 Tips and Tricks for the Highly Sensitive: How to Stay Calm in Tense Situations."

I leaf through the "Tips and Tricks". There are meditations, yoga poses, something called tapping. I get to a section on visualizations and it talks about closing your eyes and imagining walking in the woods. I stare at a picture of a forest. It's so weird to think of someone *visualizing* walking in a forest instead of just heading out the door and *walking* in a forest.

Angel stands back with her hands on her hips. "Which is it, kid? It's your choice."

My head pounds just looking at the old book. I fear if I open it, I won't be able to keep pretending, even for a minute. I point to the white one.

""Tips and Tricks' it is!" She flops the book back to Chapter 1: Breathing.

It reminds me of the ritual of breathing with Blue. Like visualizing walking in the forest, it's weird to me that humans have such a hard time remembering to breathe that someone wrote a book about it.

Angel starts reading the breathing exercises out loud. When I don't listen, she says, "Hey, kid! This is important."

I'm so tired already. Tired that we live in a world where we have to be taught how to breathe.

Angel sees the exhaustion on my face. "Ah, kid," she says and plays with my hair. Just then, a beam of light from the window catches the disco ball and stars spin around the inside of the shed.

"I don't envy you," Angel whispers, flying among the stars. "I don't envy any of the kids born now."

Chapter 14

When Aunt Angel finds out that I've never taken a bus before, she adds it to the school bootcamp. She decides we'll take the city bus...every day until school starts.

We stand in front of the totem pole at the Chamber of Commerce at the bus stop in town, and the plan is to travel to her house, 12 miles as the crow flies and 30 minutes as the bus drives. She had me write down tips and tricks on index cards that I carry in my fanny pack.

When the bus pulls up, my body is already buzzing. Even as we walk down the bus aisle between the ten or so people on the bus, I start picking up everybody's thoughts and feelings. It's so much easier in the forest when what I feel isn't pain and confusion. It's like the mall but worse because the bus is jerking and stopping and swerving and making my stomach sick.

Next to us in the seat across the aisle, a man is hunched in a brown coat. He's sleeping or sick or something. I see his life through his molasses eyes. His emotions are thick and the pictures I get are covered in dark film. It's like I'm walking deep underwater. Angel sees me staring and points to the fanny pack.

I pull out a card.

Breathe in for the count of 5, hold for 5, breathe out for 5.

I breathe and try to send my thoughts to the man so that he'll do it with me, but I can't get him to breathe.

More people get on, and the chatter makes me jumpy. I'm holding it together but then a homeless guy gets on with a beard, and I start to panic. I'm not scared of him, I'm feeling him, the pain of him, the despair, the emptiness. Angel points to my fanny pack again but I can't focus. She fumbles with the zipper to get at the cards, but it's too late.

I can't breathe. I put my head between my knees but I still can't breathe.

Angel pulls the bell, hauls me up like a sack of potatoes, and we stumble off the bus. It's raining and I feel so much relief to feel the rain on my skin. Angel starts trudging back down the hill to the car but I ask her to wait. I take my shoes off go to the grass beside the road and sink my toes into the earth. I wonder if putting your toes in the grass is one of the "Tips and Tricks". When I'm finally breathing right again, I look around. We've made it four stops, up the hill next to the vet's office. The rain grows heavier. We're sopping wet as we trudge a mile back to Angel's car.

"Sorry," I keep saying. "Sorry."

Angel doesn't answer, just holds my hand in a fierce grip.

***

More time in the shed. More tips and tricks. Two days later we're back at the bus stop. Four days and counting until school starts.

A woman on the bus cradles a chihuahua and I can feel the dog is dying. Not today, but maybe in 10 days. The woman doesn't know. She keeps calling her Baby and bouncing her in her arms, and I start crying and I can't stop crying, and Angel gives me credit because at least this time we made it eight stops.

***

We're in the shed, and crystals and candles and incense are spread like a meal across one of the tables, like a spirit feast. I can tell Angel's trying something different because the energy is different. Maybe she is casting a spell. I don't know. There's musky incense swirling everywhere, and six candles flickering, and glitter filling the whole space from the disco ball. It's a good thing Mom is still in bed because she'd have a meltdown around so much woo-woo.

I sit down and look around. "It feels like a dream today."

"Yes, perfect," Angel says, "enter the dream. It's all a dream. A forest dream, and a school dream. Let's make the dream work for us."

The book is opened to chapter 6. It's an exercise to use when you're having anxiety or panic attacks. Angel has written the exercise on the big pad of paper:

Name:

5 things you can see

4 things you can physically feel

3 things you can hear

2 things you can smell

1 thing you can taste

"It's a way to bring you back into the present moment when you're panicking," Angel says. "To help you live inside your body, and not outside it."

"I hate this," I say, quietly.

"This exercise?"

"No, this whole thing. It makes me think something is wrong with me. I'm broken and I need to be fixed. I don't feel that way with Blue."

"Maybe it's something wrong with the world. Maybe you're picking up the dis-ease of the whole wide world," Angel says. "We're just trying to figure out how to 'be' in this panicking world, OK?"

I have another problem with all of this but I don't say it to Angel. I don't understand the difference between being a sensitive person and an anxious person. One feels positive and gentle and the other like I'm not good at coping.

Is my reaction to the rest of the world sensitivity or is it anxiety? Or is Angel right, am I just picking up on everyone else's anxiety? I need to think about it.

Angel's right about one thing. I have to figure out how to survive in the real world. If I'm going to go to school and try to save at least some of the forest, I have to figure out how to *deal*.

Angel points to the pad of paper. "If we practice this, it'll be easier for you to actually do it when you're in the throes of overstimulation, OK? Let's go. Five things you can see."

"What I see," I look around. "Orange painting of Twister eating a persimmon, my untied purple tie-dyed sneaker, roll of blue tape, stringy brown dream catcher, lumpy red lava lamp."

"What I feel." I get up and move around Mom's studio, touching things. "Dried paint on palette, plastic stencil with cut-out leaves, paintbrush bristles…" I touch Apollo's nose and he sneezes. "And wet nose."

I go through the rest of them.

Hear: "Motorcycle on the far-away road, sad hawk crying, Apollo farting."

Smell: "Apollo farting! Nag champa incense."

Taste: "Rosemary lavender Kombucha"

***

I'm back at the bus stop, by myself this time because I have to prove I can do it. Angel is in the car, watching from across the road.

I'm OK for a while on the bus until a couple of high school kids in the back start throwing a tennis shoe. It's some other kid's footwear. I don't feel like the shoeless kid, and I don't feel like the bullies, I feel like the shoe. Every time they throw it, they throw me. Back and forth. Back and forth.

I stare out the window and try naming things I can see and hear and taste and feel, but the first thing I see is too upsetting. They're cutting down so many forests. Mom and I had already talked about this on our long drives together. So many forests in our county are being cut down to plant Christmas tree farms. "Polyculture being destroyed to be replaced with a monoculture," Mom explained. When I look out the window of the bus, I see the price tags hanging from the trees of the forests that are left and force my eyes close so I don't burst into tears.

I take a card from my fanny pack—a hodge-podge list of lots of different tips, or maybe they're tricks.

Count all of the blue things I see.

Four!

Name them.

Blue car. Blue sign. Blue door. Blue shirt.

Find all the things that start with C.

Car. Clock. Curtains. Crossroad. Cat.

I realize suddenly I'm halfway to Angel's. I'm going to make it!

At the next stop, a dozen screaming preschoolers get on all tied together with a rope. It's not like there is any darkness coming from the kids. They're like bright beads on a necklace, all different colors in their rain slickers and bright rain boots. What people don't understand is that it doesn't have to be bad to be overwhelming. Even good stuff can be too much. It's their noise. It's like I'm a musical instrument and every screech from them is someone plucking my strings. Before I know it, I'm off the bus and standing at the side of the highway, trying to breathe.

Angel pulls up in the car. She's been following the bus.

I open the passenger door and say, "I'll try again tomorrow."

She looks at me, hard. She holds my hand all the way home.

***

It's one day before school. I wake before the sun rises and run to Blue and lean my face against her. I adjust the scarves around her waist. Before Mom took to her bed, we gathered all of our scarves – we had lots of them between us, stripes and flowers and polka dots – and we tied them together until they reached around Blue's middle.

"What am I going to do, Blue? I'm never going to make it."

I feel myself falling. Blue expands around me and over me until her bark becomes my skin. I feel spongy inside, but hard and protected on the outside.

Blue knows. She knows.

I just need her bark.

On the way to the house, I hear a big machine noise from the street. The driveway is too long for me to see what it is. I sit in the corner of the porch and hold my knees. It's the loggers, I know it is. I wait. But nothing comes.

***

That day on the city bus, I'm alone again. Angel drove me to the bus stop "It's do or die, kid," she said. "If you don't make it this time, no school." She's not following the bus this time but has driven on to her house where she's waiting. Today *has* to work.

A little girl next to me has a hard candy, and she's crinkling the plastic. She's not opening it to eat it, just playing with it. I read the girl's mind. I get a clear picture of what she's thinking.

The candy is from her grandmother, and she's thinking about her grandmother's crooked toes, and how her mom has to fit her slippers over them, and how grandmother always gives her candy and she never eats them but keeps them in a bowl on her dresser.

Breathe.

Three things I can hear, crinkly candy plastic, a snoring man behind me, bus revving.

Before the start of this journey, I put a piece of Blue's bark in my pocket. I take it out now and trace the roughness with my fingers, put the bark to my cheek, and smell it.

I look up and realize. I've gone further than ever before. *Patchouli on the girl in tie-dye, Chinese food in a bag on a man's lap, orange lotion on the woman in front of me.*

We pass a sign that says the name of Angel's town! Angel bought me a cell phone for school, in case of emergencies. I text her and tell her where I am. *I'm coming. I'm coming.*

She texts back two hands praying and fingers crossed.

The little girl looks at me and hands me the hard candy. I smile and take it, unwrap it, and pop it in my mouth.

One thing I can taste: *Sour tart lemon.*

The bus turns onto Angel's street. She's standing at the bus stop in a bright yellow muumuu. She stretches out her arms when she sees my face pressed to the window. She looks like the sun.

I ding the bell. The bus stops. I stand at the doorway.

"Kid, you did it!" Angel cries.

I stumble down the stairs, run to her, and fall into her arms. I'm a baby who's just learned to walk.

Chapter 15

Mom's shadow is the shadow of the loggers, of the crazy wind, of the smoke of wildfires. Mom's darkness isn't just her own. Her whole body is a sponge and she sucks up everything that happens around her. In this world, that's a lot of heaviness to have in your body.

I love her for this, for being open and caring. I want to protect her from this. I am the Keeper of the Forest and the Keeper of the Mother.

But I'm also upset. It's the first day of school and I'm standing in her dark room. She has the blanket up over her head. Now? This has to happen now? Who even cares that I'm going to school for the first time *ever*, the loggers will be here any day. We have to pay attention!

"Mom?" I whisper. "I'm going to school now." She's so deep in her shadow coma, that I'm not sure she hears me. The only lights are thin lines that shine through narrow slits in the blinds.

"Mo-om, did you hear me?" I turn on the light. She groans and burrows.

"Maisie," she says, her voice muffled inside the covers. "Please please turn off the light."

I switch it off.

Angel has already been in here trying to get her up. She's also been calling the bookstore where they work, making sure Mom has a job to go back to. This dark room has happened before and it will happen again. Once, they almost took me away. Once we almost lost everything. The house. The forest. Each other. Since then, we have tried to keep it all to ourselves, Angel, me, and Mom.

As I stare at the mound beneath the blankets, and smell the tangy sick room, I feel my stomach buzzing. I realize Mom is scaring me as much as the loggers, as much as school. *I'm scared, Mom! Mom? Mom?*

I don't say anything, just stare at the mound that is my mother. I understand something else then. I realize she was right. I *do* need to get out of this house and away from her. I *do* need to find others.

As I leave the room, I hear muffled words and soft crying. "I'm sorry. I'm so sorry..."

***

On the front porch, Angel looks me up and down. She stands tall and gives me an exaggerated salute. I come to attention and salute her back. We're sergeant and soldier and I'm off to battle.

"LaForet, where's your uniform?" she barks.

I look down at my clothes—rainbows, flowers, and polka dots.

She straightens my shirt, "Didn't Sara buy you new clothes for school?"

"I don't feel like *me* in them."

"Quite right! Well done, Private. We're entering a new battle and only those soldiers willing to be themselves will conquer all." She reaches into her Mary Poppins bag and pulls something out. She bows and extends her hand. "A gift for the drafted soldier." On her palm sits a tiny box wrapped in a brown paper sack.

I grab it and open it. "Air pods." I don't know what they are. She takes the box from me excitedly, opens it, takes out each pod, and puts them in my ears.

"Another tool for your toolbox. A lot of my highly sensitive clients swear by these." She reaches into my pocket and takes my phone. "I found this music when you were sleeping last night and uploaded it to your phone. You can listen on the bus or between classes."

With a dramatic arc of her arm, she hits play.

"They took the rings of trees and created an algorithm and then set the trees to piano music," Angel says and looks at my phone. "This one is an ash tree. Whadaya think?!"

The sounds are inside me, a mix of classical and jazz, pounding keys then a single note. Something about it is familiar. My body buzzes.

This is the sound of the rings of an ash tree? My heart pounds. It's like hearing Blue. I can barely breathe. I tear them out of my ears.

"You don't like it? How can you not like it, kid?" she asks. "Try a different tree. There are all kinds of trees on here." She tries to take the ear pods from me and stick them back in my ears. I veer away.

"No!"

"What?"

She of all people should understand. I've told her before. Stuff doesn't have to be *bad* to be *overwhelming*.

I put the pods in my pocket. "I gotta get to the bus stop," I say, and start down the driveway. She follows. "Look, I need to walk up the driveway to the bus stop by myself," I tell her.

"Your Ma wants a picture of you getting on the bus," she says.

"No!" I scream.

She stops. "OK, I get it, kid." She stands to attention, clicks her heels, nose up, and salutes me.

I salute back and turn back to the driveway. After several feet, I turn around and she's back on the porch watching me.

The clouds are wild and big. Today smoke lingers in the air, but it isn't bad. I often sing to the trees and critters when I go up to get the mail, but today all I can do is whisper—to the birches, the bunnies, the abandoned Christmas tree lot, "Goodbye. I'll be back. I promise." I can't see Blue from up here but I blow her a kiss. "Watch for the loggers for me, Blue," I whisper.

This is the first transition from home to school. I'm trying to turn my mind over as I walk, to shift my thoughts from house to bus. This journey feels scary and big and the opposite of what I want. Everything in me is telling me to turn back. *Nothing good can come out of this! It's all going to be too overwhelming! You won't survive it!*

I keep going.

At the top of the driveway, the school bus stop is a patch of grass at the side of the road—on both sides are fields, hills, and forests. I stop when I see a woman standing there. What's a grown woman doing at the school bus stop?

As I get closer, I see it's Macon George, my neighbor. She's my age. The last time I saw her she was normal sized. But I don't see her much. Mom keeps me away from the George family. "Different politics" is the only reason she'll give.

Macon has thighs now and breasts. Even wearing overalls, you can see how curvy and grown-up she is. She folds herself so she doesn't draw attention, and I can tell she doesn't have any idea how beautiful she is.

She sees me looking at her body and blushes. I look down at my flat chest and blush.

"Hey," she says.

"Hey."

We stand side by side. She's more than a foot taller than me. We fidget quietly until the bus comes five minutes later.

Macon gets on first. I follow, but by the time I've gone only a few steps, I'm hit with a wall of screaming kids and my body begins to crumble. This is worse than the city bus. How could it be *worse*?

I fumble in the earbuds, praying a singing ash tree will be less overwhelming than one zillion hollering kids.

I'm not on the bus yet, and already I'm fried.

Chapter 16

Let's just say the school bus is nothing like the city bus. Let's just say I'm hunched over my phone reading the tips and tricks, and under my breath and behind my hair I'm naming, and breathing, and visualizing. Let's just say, nothing is working.

And we're not even at the next bus stop yet!

The bus does pull over and I'm ready to jump and run, when I look up and realize we're at the Watanabes. I peer out and see Jack. Jack? Here? But why am I surprised? Of course, she'd be on the bus. She goes to school. How could I have not thought about that?

Jack.

My best friend.

Jaqueline.

Ur, former best friend. And *never* call her Jaqueline.

I'm in the last seat and the back door opens, and something starts whirring, and it takes me a second to realize that the wheelchair lift is at the back of the bus. As the lift comes back up, JAX appears inch by inch. Before she sees me, I study her. How much she's changed in three years. Her black hair is long now, with braids that reach her lap, a purple streak through the right braid, thick eyeliner drawn at angles, an armband with spikes on it. She's a few years older, and even though she's skinny, she's even more grown-up looking than Macon. But, of course, she would be. Because of the accident, she was held back a grade. She's a year older, 12 now. I wonder if she still does art like she used to. She used to carry a journal everywhere and draw everything. My heart burns with seeing her.

Then she sees me.

"Jack," I whisper.

She scowls. "It's JAX now. All caps!"

The way she's looking at me, I want to jump through the back door and run home. I want to hug her. I want to hide. All of the feelings.

Much much.

Up until three years ago, Jack, I mean JAX, and I were inseparable. We'd draw in her room, dress up for Halloween, play in my forest – this was before the accident. Then she threw me out of her bedroom and told me to not ever come back. She was right to throw me out. That's why I never even tried to go back. She was right.

"What are *you* doing here?" she barks.

"Going to school?" I say too loud and too high pitched, like it's a question, like I want her permission, like I'm hoping she'll say *No, you're not* so I can get off this crazy merry-go-round and go home.

JAX rolls her eyes. The bus driver lumbers down the aisle and straps in her chair. I stare at her trying to figure out what to say.

"Quit staring like I'm some kind of freak," she hisses.

I want to say, *No, No, that's not it,* but I'm frozen and she won't look at me and it's hopeless.

I look at her again, and then again, but she won't look back, so I give up.

***

The bus is stopping and starting, stopping and starting. So many kids. So much noise.

Inhale one two three four five.

Hold one two three four five.

Exhale one two three four five.

Face plastered to window: *Open sky, fields of tree stubs, dusty brown soil, Christmas tree farm, Christmas tree farm, Christmas tree farm. Forests gone. All gone. Blue! Blue!*

I blast the Air pods, Cottonwood like a dozen popping water balloons.

A boy stands in the aisle next to my seat motioning with his arms.

My heart sinks. It's a kid named Will. I was part of his play group when I was really little. He's a nightmare.

"You kids stay in your seats," the bus driver yells, but Will doesn't listen.

"Oh no way, it's Clown girl! Clown girl!" he bellows. He reaches and ruffles my hair. "Clown girl is here!"

I sink down on the seat. He gave me the nickname in our playgroup it stuck. I'm praying it doesn't stick here. JAX, Will, Macon...I guess I didn't realize going to school meant that every kid I never really wanted to see would be all in one place.

"Will, beat it!" JAX yells. I look at her surprised. Is she protecting me? She still won't meet my eye.

"Whatever," Will says, using his fingers to make an L on his forehead as he turns and heads back up the aisle.

I turn toward JAX. I want to tell her about the logging, about Blue and the scarves. I want to tell her about Mom in the bedroom, and how I leave soup on the side table but she won't eat. I used to tell JAX my dreams. She never doubted them. She saw them come true. She used to call me MG instead of Maisie-Grace. She also called me Psycho Kid. Not psychic kid, Psycho Kid. I feel it's urgent that I tell her. I need help, and I don't know why I think she could possibly help me.

My throat locks.

"What??" she says, looking defiantly at me.

I turn back around without saying a word.

Meanwhile, there's some big commotion up at the front of the bus with Will. I take out the earbuds. Will's standing beside Macon.

"*Bacon* just fell out of your pocket," Will yells.

"Settle down!" the bus driver yells.

"Who carries *bacon* in their pocket? Oh my God, loooooooooooooser!" Will holds up an L. "Ma-con. Ba-con," he sings. "Ma-con. Ba-con."

Others join in.

"Ma-con. Ba-con."

"Ma-con. Ba-con."

"You kids sit down and keep it quiet!" the bus driver yells again. Nobody listens.

"Ma-con. Ba-con," they chant.

"Shut up!" JAX yells. "Shut up! Shut up!" It's too loud. Nobody can hear her. "Normals," she fumes. It's her biggest insult. JAX always hated anything and anyone who was normal.

I look out the window ready to pop from all of the chaos, and then sit up surprised. The bus is pulling into the school parking lot. We're here!

"I made it! I made it!" I bounce on my seat and turn to JAX. "I made it!"

She scowls and turns away.

Chapter 17

The first day of school is a blur. Teeming hallways, new faces, teachers, textbooks, thoughts and feelings bouncing off lockers and walls and bodies.

My lights dim, my off switch flips.

Beep.

Fog.

This off switch I have—I can't control it. It happens when I'm overwhelmed. Noise becomes soft and faraway, desks and people and walls take on dreamy shapes and vague colors. I float outside my body.

I smile.

I nod.

Everybody seems to think I'm fine. Apparently, I'm a pleasure to be around when my switch is off.

I go in and out of the fog. Sometimes I'm awake, sometimes I'm not. Somehow, I figure out which classes to go to. In the background, they're ticking off the rules, so many rules – raising hands, and sitting down, so much sitting for so many hours, and bells telling you when to go, locker combinations, and other rules too, like how to talk to other kids, and who you can talk to, and why. I feel like I'm floating near the ceiling and watching it all from above. I know I need to pay more attention, but I can't get back into my body.

***

Sometime during the day, I awaken to someone tapping me on the back. I open and close my eyes, unable to figure out where I am. A tree is singing in my ear. Maybe I'm in the forest.

Again, the tapping on my back. Tap. Tap. Tap.

I blink and realize my head is between my knees. I sit up. I reach out my hand to steady myself and grab a toilet roll holder. I think I'm in the forest and I expect to touch bark, but instead feel metal and paper. I realize I'm in a bathroom stall.

Someone clears their throat.

I glance up. Macon George is standing at the doorway. She says something but I can't hear her because a Weeping Willow is screaming into my ears at maximum volume. I fumble the earbuds out.

"What?"

"I just asked if you're OK?" Macon yells as if she's screaming at a deaf person.

Just peachy, I don't say.

"Mr. Arnold sent me in to see what happened because you've been in the bathroom forever."

Mr. Arnold? I try to remember. Science. Right? Is that right? Macon is so tall in the doorway, like a monster, her shadow looming over me. I feel like I'm in an old Grimm fairy tale and I want to get out of it, but the fog in my brain is too thick. I start hyperventilating. I can't breathe.

Macon studies me. "Did you know that animals get freaked out sometimes, too?" Her family owns a farm. The few times I have seen her, she's always out feeding the pigs or with the goats.

"OK?"

"I figured out a way to calm them down," she says.

"Oh," I wheeze.

"Can I do it to you?"

"Uh," I reply in a high-pitched wheeze.

She gets on her knees on the dirty tiles, lifts my left foot, takes my shoe off. Does the same to my right foot. She holds the bottom of my socked feet in her hands. "That's all. Just like this," she says.

And in a minute, I do calm down.

The school bell rings, and we both jump. There's a rush of commotion in the hallways outside the bathroom door.

"We have to get to assembly," Macon says. "Come on. Then we can go home."

***

Macon sticks by my side like glue, like a huge protector. Will tries to rub my head, yelling "clown girl", but she shoves him away. We join hundreds of other kids on the bleachers.

They're calling it a Welcome Assembly. The principal is at the podium, grey hair and stooped shoulders. I don't know what's welcoming about any of it, because he seems to be talking about guns and shooters. The way his voice shakes when he says "gun" and "active shooter" and "drills". And how this week we'll be practicing how not to get shot.

I think: *Great, another super awesome reason for me to be at school.*

Beep.

Fog.

***

When I come to the next time, I'm home, in the forest, curled in Blue's roots. I wake up and there's a light branch with a spray of needles covering me like a blanket. I don't know if it's a dream. Is Blue the dream? Is school the dream?

I move the branch, scramble up, and rub my palms over Blue's bark. I *am* home

Breathe with me, Blue says.

I see a lunchbox tucked behind one of the roots and recognize it as Macon's. I open it, and inside is a Twinkie, a candy bar, a soda – all the stuff Mom would never let me have. I devour the

Twinkie, chug the soda. I vaguely remember Macon walking me down the driveway, and me leading her to Blue.

I stand up and glance around. There is still no sign of the loggers. It's almost dark. I take my boots and socks off, sit in the dirt, dig my toes in. I put my hands flat on the earth. I sit this way until the sun goes down.

I know I have to get back up to the house. I don't know if Angel knows I'm down here, or if she's already sent a posse out looking for me. I trudge up through the young forest and notice her car is gone.

Inside, there's a note on the kitchen table.

"Kid, my sister's in the hospital. I gotta go catch a flight. I'll call you when I can. Remember, school will get better. I promise. Hate leaving you and your Ma like this. I called my neighbor, Constance, and she's gonna come check in on you. I hate doing this, but I gotta go."

Who is this Constance? I don't even recognize the name. I feel sick. Why did Angel bring another person into this? It isn't safe.

I warm up a can of soup for dinner and take a bowl into Mom's room. She turns toward me, and croaks, "You're home." I wait for her to ask about school, but she turns her face away.

The phone rings, and it's Constance. I lie and tell her Mom is better and there's no need to worry or to come by or to call. I get off the phone fast before she starts asking questions.

I go to the living room. Grab the binoculars. I pace back and forth, binoculars to my face, waiting for the loggers.

Chapter 18

School doesn't get better. The second day is worse than the first, the third worse than all of them. The chaos builds until my insides tumble, and I don't know up from down or left from right. I walk the halls and go to class and it's like living inside a foggy kaleidoscope, color fragments and splintered movements.

I keep messing up the rules. I've never had to sit so long in my life. Mom made me study much harder than this...and we had a walking classroom, a kayaking classroom, a snow shoeing classroom. I don't understand how people think they can learn anything sitting in a room every day.

It's all so easy. Even in a fog, I know the answers, and say them without raising my hand because I keep forgetting the rules. *"Miss LaForet, you need to raise your hand." "Miss Laforet, I didn't give you permission to leave your desk." "Miss LaForet, quit talking."*

"Sit!"

"Sit down."

"Down! Down!"

It only takes me a few days – even with my switch off – to figure out it's a game, and you just have to learn the rules and play. Sit. Stand. Walk. Sit. Reply. Do homework. Smile. Nod. Bobblehead doggie.

What I see, what I understand, even when I'm only half there is how much everybody is pretending. I can see the kids' souls and nearly everyone is pretending. In my fog, my master pretender has taken over, and because everybody is sort of pretending, that's why nobody notices.

I see through everybody. This is the most overwhelming thing of all. I see who they are, but because they're all pretending (and sometimes they don't even *know* they're pretending), it takes a while for me to figure out how to talk to them. If I speak to who they really are, a lot of times it scares them or upsets them. So, most of the time, I just keep my mouth shut. Unless I forget.

I see:

Will's dad is beating the crap out of him. He's pretending to be tough, but really, he's broken.

JAX is so angry it's like a black wall you can't see around. It's like she's a cave filled with jewels but the opening to the cave is sealed up.

Macon is a beautiful girl who thinks she has a big ugly body, but really her body is stunning. She's a gentle soul trapped in a harsh family. She's not pretending, she's just going so far inward maybe she'll never get out again.

I can see the teachers, too. I can see the ones who believe in teaching and want to change the world, who—even if they're exhausted—still care. I see the teachers who don't care, the angry ones. There's one teacher who isn't good, who has bad intentions, who reminds me of my dad. Mom thinks because we left before I was five that I don't remember my father, but I do. I remember everything.

The bad teacher is scary. Are people pretending not to see it, or do they really not see? How do I possibly tell people about him? The English teacher, Mr. Altishin, has a poster in his classroom, "If you see something, say something." But what if you have a way of seeing that nobody believes? What if see things that haven't happened yet? What then?

I start asking to go to the bathroom in each class and sit in a stall with my head between my knees, trying to read tips and tricks on my phone upside down.

Every once in a while, I come out of it. It's like I wake up from a dream for a few minutes then fall asleep again.

In the cafeteria, I'm sitting with JAX and I don't know why since she hates me. Macon is there, feeding me carrot sticks from my own lunch bag like I'm a rabbit.

Beep.

Fog.

Mr. Altishin, gives us tattered paperbacks. I come to looking down at the book in my hand. In it is Dogsong by Gary Paulsen, one of my favorites because it has a Shaman and I think maybe school won't be so bad, maybe it will be OK, but...

Beep.

Fog.

In Math, I wake up and the teacher is standing over my shoulder looking at my work. I look down at my notebook, and realize even in a fog I can do math. She says, "Miss LaForet, see me after class," and everybody looks at me like deer in headlights. After class, the teacher says, "You're too advanced for this class. I'm moving you," and I think, even in a fog, I can succeed. Even as a bobblehead dog I can make it, and this scares me. And then I walk out of the classroom into the hallway and I'm hit by a wall of chaos.

Beep.

Fog.

***

I feel the plop, plop, plop of water and open my eyes. Big raindrops drip onto my cheek. I'm curled in Blue's roots again. The rain hums as it pours down in fat sheets, but Blue's canopy keeps me from getting completely drenched.

The fourth day of school, and it still isn't any easier. I start to tell Blue, and I'm looking around as I'm speaking, and something is different about the forest.

"Why does the forest look different, Blue?" I ask.

Blue is silent, scary quiet.

It's the mud. There's a big mud path in front of Blue, starting at the edge of the forest and running a couple hundred yards up the hill. I sink my foot into the mud. Not just mud, a path. Not just a path, a road. I walk it, barefoot, mud like brown socks up to my ankles. Where there used to be shrubs, blackberry vines, ferns, and a narrow foot path, there is now a big fat muddy road. I shake my head. Close and open my eyes. The road is still there.

I want to believe this is a dream, but my shoes are off, and mud is squeezing up between my toes, and I'm running up the muddy road in the shoveling rain.

I follow the new road up. It's not just the tall grass that's gone. The path was lined with stray trees, and some of the limbs have been ripped out and torn off. There's nothing gentle about this. The muddy road connects with our gravel driveway at the top of the hill. A big red machine with a claw is tucked back between some brush. My foggy brain finally clicks – this is a *logging road*! They put in a logging road while I was at school. My body starts to vibrate and I can't stop shaking.

"Blue?" I cry, running back to her, wanting to hug her, to open my arms and hug the big sheets of rain, to hold it all, to protect it all. How can I be Keeper of the Forest? What can I do?

Breathe with me, Blue says.

"No," I cry. "I'm not breathing. I'm done breathing!" And I turn, and rip up through the forest of the young trees to the house.

When I get to the yard, I stand in the rain. I can see Mom through the living room window. She's up. She's in a torn T-shirt and sweatpants. Her hair is matted to one side. I get closer to the window. She's on the sofa, sitting up but looking like it's taking all her effort not to fall sideways. The window is open a crack, and I can hear that she's on the phone with Angel.

"...pull her out. You should see her, Ange. She came into my room and she's a *zombie*.... It's my fault. I'm a horrible mother. I'm pulling her out of school."

She's clutching her coffee cup, her knuckles white. She turns and sees me.

"Maisie-Grace!" she yells. "She's back. I'll call you later." She hangs up and stumbles outside into the front yard into the pouring rain and smashes me in a bear hug. The rain is so relentless it lays upon both of our bodies like a heavy sopping blanket.

"You never have to go to school again!" she cries. "I'm sorry. I'm sorry. I'm sorry." She's squeezing so hard I can't breathe. "Horrible. Horrible." It's like the fear is leaving her body and traveling into mine. I pull away.

"No, I'm going to school." I swipe my sopping hair out of my face, and can't believe the words coming out of my mouth. "School isn't that awful," I lie.

She tries to take my face so she can look into my eyes. "You can't even function."

"Yeah, Mom, *I'm* the one who can't function."

Her face falls. She sloshes back into the house, and I follow her. She goes to the bathroom, comes back out in a robe, and hands me a towel.

"I guess it's up to you," she says, her hand too heavy on my shoulder. She goes to her bedroom and closes the door.

Don't worry, I can do it, I cry to the closed door without saying a word. *Just give me some time. I'll save us all.*

I'm a master. I can pretend.

MACON

Chapter 19

Oinks and squawks and bleats and moos and different smells of poo. I'm not supposed to name them, Dad does *not* like it, but they're Walnut and Anastasia and Goat and Jinx and Barney. And Johnny. But he died.

And it's pouring rain and they're rolling in the mud and *everybody* underestimates them. Will can "oink" at me all he wants but a pig is a thousand times smarter than he is. And Olaf barks and wiggles under the fencing and gets into the pen and he's rolling in the mud with the pigs and I wish I was an animal so I could roll, too.

And I can see down the hill between the trees and Maisie-Grace and her Mom are tiny dots in their front yard, just standing there without raincoats, and it looks like her mom is hugging her. No one in my house hugs.

Dad calls them "hippies" and I think I wish I was a hippie for a day just to get a hug. And that first day at the bus stop Maisie-Grace with her clothes so wild, so as far as I can tell, hippie means fun clothes and hugs in the front yard and maybe no brothers and no dad.

She was in the woods, once, Maisie-Grace, when I was with Johnny and I squatted and watched, and it was like a fairy tale, like she was a tree, but that doesn't make any sense because she was twirling and singing. And I thought about myself doing this, just hanging out in the forest and singing, and how my brothers would beat the crap out of me if they found me doing it. Because around here if you're outside, you're feeding or fixing fences or loading hay. You're *not* playing.

***

Oh Jinx! I'm filling the trough with the hose, and Jinx is running through the hose water, back and forth, Walnut too, squealing like kids in a sprinkler. Goat puts her snout in the gushing hose, in and out and in and out. And how each one of them is like a person, Jinx, bossy. Goat, goofy. Anastasia, little miss princess. Walnut, stubborn. Barney, soooo lazy.

How Maisie's laugh is like a wind chime and how their house is green and small and how there's this half circle of yard that's mowed but surrounded by a half acre of scrub. And how Dad goes on about it, *Somebody needs to clean up that property! Somebody needs to fix that shed! It ain't even their house!*

Mom yells out the window and I hose Olaf and collect eggs, and take off my raincoat and waders and step inside, and every burner of the stove is going, potatoes boiling, and unfortunately, pork chops and bacon frying and I try not to cry.

I don't know what happened, but the smell of pork. Woof! It's not good to love animals, not good not OK not accepted, and anyway, you fall in love and every few months they're slaughtered and it's just one heartbreak after another. And when we were in the cafeteria, I saw that Maisie-Grace never had meat in her lunch, and I wondered if she didn't eat animals, and I wanted to know more but she was pretty messed up so I couldn't ask.

Dad and the boys bust through the back door, and the whole room changes. Now, we are their servants, Mom and me. We fill plates and glasses and run here and there as they sit. Men do the outdoor work and women do the indoor work, and I'd rather be outside more, but Mom says that's just not the way it's done.

We pray and arms fly. The boys are ferocious. We butcher our own chickens and once I counted and each of my brothers and Dad ate an entire chicken. An entire chicken each!

"You'd better eat that pork today!" Dad hollers, and I stare at the four hopeless bacon strips spread across my plate. "Eat 'em, Macon! None of this nonsense." When Dad hollers your whole body vibrates but I'm more sick with the idea of eating them than in fear of him, and he's very very scary.

And I wait til he's distracted, and I do this all the time, and sometimes I don't get caught, and I slip them off my plate, wrap them in a napkin, and put them in my pocket.

And of course, I think about the first day of school when I forgot to get rid of the bacon in my pocket and I think of Will, and why do people have to be so mean all of the time, but I think more about Maisie-Grace and her rainbows and polka dots and lemon scarf that flops down to her purple boots. The Laforets are not from around here. Everybody here is big and strong like a donkey, but they're thin and tiny. And I just want to swoop in and protect her, but I stand back and nod.

But at school, I'm watching her to make sure she's OK, because the first week she isn't. You could almost think she was OK, how she kept her head down and smiled and nodded, but I know something is really wrong.

And that first day in the cafeteria, she was falling down, not on the outside but on the inside, so I steered her to the table I shared with JAX, and JAX was like shaking her head *No, No,* but I ignored her because I knew they used to be friends, but I didn't know what happened.

And she couldn't seem to eat, Maisie-Grace, so I helped her and JAX kept looking so upset, and I wanted her to be OK too, but I didn't know what was going on.

And Mr. Anderson the science teacher tells me to go find Maisie-Grace, and I find her in the bathroom stall and she's so tiny and pretty and I feel so huge, like a big fumbling galoot, and she's bent over with her head between her knees. And I think about Jinx...maybe her being at school is like if I bring

Jinx to school and expect him to be happy with floor tiles and no mud. Like Maisie Grace was a tree without a forest.

As I kneel and hold her feet and they're so tiny and she has on rainbow socks and I think sometimes the whole world just needs someone to hold their feet.

JAX

Chapter 20

She's like an infection, like a cold sore on my brain, *Get out of my head! Get out! Get out!*

And now she's on my ceiling.

I'm in bed and the plaster above my head is moving and shifting and images are appearing. I always see my art this way, first on my bedroom ceiling, and then I go to my art table and paint. It started after the accident during rehab when I couldn't get out of bed by myself and I'd stare at that ceiling for hours, days, months.

For an eternity.

The first images to appear were of the accident, running like a movie. Rewind. Replay. Rewind. Replay. Until my head was going to implode.

Then the pictures started to change. I saw friends flying around the ceiling, and whirling and dancing –- people who had nothing to do with the crash. So, I started sketching them, painting them. When Dad looks at my art now, he says: "Jaja-chan, before you were good at drawing, after you become artist."

Then over the months, the figures started to sprout capes and become superheroes. Every morning there was a different superhero for me to draw. I had the idea that each one had a superpower and each one a fatal flaw. Their power was something they had that could change the world, and their fatal flaw was something that could kill them. There has to be a fatal flaw because without it, with just a superpower – BORING! There has to be something dark because everything in the world is so dark, and people are so dark, but they act like they're all just light and stuff and just showing the nice stuff is like putting pink icing on rotten cupcakes.

So, I give the drawings superhero names with their power and their fatal flaw. Like my PT Joanne. She's a horse, the way she works my arms and legs, like I'm a wounded foal. I can tell sometimes she's really depressed. She moves so slowly like she's trying to walk through molasses. This darkness is her fatal flaw. So, I call her "Dark Horse".

And then there's Macon George, who hovers around me at school. "The Protector" I call her. She's on my wall with her animal fur cape. She's always hunched and looks dumpy when really, she's beautiful. Her dumpiness is why people keep dumping on her.

I call her "Dumpy Protector".

Every day, I set the alarm for six for "ceiling time" so I have time to draw before school, but over the past few days... Who's flying across my ceiling? *Her.*

Not flying. Twirling.

MG.

Insert frustrated eyeroll here.

I shut and open and shut and open my eyes but it doesn't make any difference. It's her. Red hair. Crazy clothes. Polka dot rainboots.

I don't want it. I don't want to draw her. I don't want to *feel*.

I.

Do.

Not.

Want.

To!

I look at my phone—7 a.m. I have to get to the art table. This is when I draw what I've seen on the ceiling. I don't want to but I realize it'll bother me all day if I don't, and maybe this will purge her from my system. This is when I go to my art table and draw whatever I've seen on the ceiling.

I sit up and swing my legs over the side of the bed.

Except my legs don't swing.

Sometimes I forget. I forget even more horrible things too, until it all comes rushing back like a tsunami.

My clothes are on the edge of the bed where I put them last night. It's best to get dressed before I get into the chair. The T-shirt's easy. A skull and cross bones on it. Poison.

I grab the black jeans, lift my left foot with one hand, and put it in the pant leg. Then I lift the other foot and place it in the other side. I move the jeans up each leg with my hands. Rolling my upper body until I'm on my stomach, I pull them over my butt.

Everything takes ten times as long as before. Black socks, combat boots, leather studded choker, studded armband, skull earrings.

"Jaja-chan," Dad yells from outside the door. "Do you need help with braiding hair?"

"I'm good, Dad," I yell back. He's had to learn a lot more than braiding since Mom died. He's bent over now. He shuffles now—like an old man, like he grew old overnight.

I use my hand to swing one leg then the other off the side of the bed. I always leave the chair facing the end table. Gripping the edge of the seat, I hoist myself over.

Sometimes I miss, face planting on the carpet. Dad runs in all flustered. *Don't do it by yourself, JaJa-chan.*

I keep doing it anyway.

I have to.

Over to my art table. Dad has bought me so many art supplies over the years that I could open an art store. Tubs and boxes and vases full of markers, brushes, tubes. K-POP on my phone, the ceiling image takes me over like I'm possessed. I seem to have no choice. My hands have a mind of their own. They fly across the art paper.

Markers, colored pencils, stencils, paints, brushes.

Corkscrew hair, wild clothes, the boots.

I don't know. I'm not in charge here.

Whatever is controlling me is making me use color. Lots of color. I prefer black. Tacked up all over the room are black ink portraits, of Dad, of Mom, of friends, a few of the teachers.

But now, I'm using neon greens, lemon yellows, turquoise blues. Color is for amateurs. Color is for normals. And for the past several months, I hate to admit it to myself, but color has been coming into my artwork, a lot! Too much.

If I see it on the ceiling, I can't control it. I find my hands grabbing the paints and colored markers and I can't stop them.

MG's cape is covered with forest. As she twirled across the ceiling, the cape picked up dark green leaves and antelope brown twigs and burnt umber fir cones, until the cape was swishing with the woods, until nature was surrounding her like a cloud.

Even as my hands go crazy and fast with the image, I don't like the feeling. Drawing is so intimate. It's like you fall in love with the thing you're drawing, like you get to know it better than it knows itself.

I finish, hold it up. It's whimsical, silly, and childlike. I want it to be blacker, grayer, more goth.

"Psycho," I say. That's her greatest strength. She talks to trees and dreams and reads your mind. Maybe it's also her fatal flaw. I sit staring at it. Is her strength her fatal flaw, too? No, that's not it. Rage washes through me. I pick up a dark marker and add a gag to cover her mouth.

"Gagged Psycho," I say out loud.

I look at the drawing and want to tear it to pieces. It takes everything in me not to shred it with my nails. I roll over to my closet, open the doors.

The closet no longer holds clothes. I took all of the shirts and pants out and stuffed them in the dresser. Inside closet is my secret gallery. This is where I hide the colorful artwork. There are about a dozen now, hanging on the back wall. No one, and I mean no one, has ever seen this art. It's so girlie. Too girlie. Fatal.

I remember reading once that Stephen King wished he was a different kind of author. He wished the stories that came through him weren't horror stories. I feel the same about this art in the closet.

I tape MG to the inside walls with the rest of them. I close the closet doors.

MG lingers with me as I get ready for school.

I don't like the feeling.

I can't let her in again.

I won't.

I set my jaw. *OK, I've drawn you, Gagged Psycho, but I won't forgive you.*

Not after what you did.

Not after what you didn't *do.*

MAISIE-GRACE

Chapter 21

In Social Studies I wake up.

Blue taught me once to look for the light. When something is meant for you, it'll be surrounded by light. *Follow the light, child,* Blue says, *Always follow the light.* The teacher is Miss Sullivan.

She's glowing.

She's black and muscular, her dreadlocks tied in a thick ponytail. When she calls my name and looks at me, it's like she reaches down inside me and pulls me to the surface. I watch her calling other kids' names and how she reaches into them and pulls them up, too. One by one, I watch her wake up the others, and I think, *I'm not the only one in a fog here. Maybe, we're all in a fog.*

She paces the front of the classroom, staring out the window and I can read her mind and know she just wants to be outside, just wants to hike and climb rocks and hang out on rivers.

Brandishing a marker like a sword, she writes on the whiteboard: ACTIVISM. It's our second class with her. I've been going crazy waiting for it. I know in my gut there's something here that can help Blue.

"What is activism?" she asks. She paces. "I'll tell you what activism is not. It isn't a meme. It's not getting likes on social media."

She puts her hand to her heart.

"Passion." She pumps her hands like it's her heart beating. "Passion." It's like she's singing. "We love, and things are unfair and we can't keep quiet. The wrong just makes you crazy. You *have* to do something."

She points at the word on the whiteboard.

"'What is Activism?' is the single most important question. That's the question we'll keep coming back to. What is it? How do we do it? Why? When? Where? How?"

"Examples of activism, please! Shout them out."

Kids yell:

"Portland protests!"

"Saving the whales!"

"Pro-life!"

"Climate change!"

"Butterflies!"

"Gun control!" one girl yells.

"Gun rights!" Will yells louder.

I'm going back into the fog, so I reach down and pinch my thigh. *Stay. Stay.*

"You can be an activist, here and now. You don't have to go anywhere. You don't have to take a plane to help the poor in Africa. You don't have to take care of the world. Focus on your patch of earth. That's what we're going to talk about." She writes the word ACTION underneath ACTIVISM.

This is why I'm here, I think. This is why I had to go to school. This is how I'm going to save the forest.

Under ACTIVISM and ACTION, she writes: COMMUNITY.

"Community is another keyword. Write it down." I do. "What is a community?" she asks.

I yell out: "Forest!"

"Beautiful," she says. She looks at the seating chart. "Maisie-Grace LaForet, exactly. Good." She smiles and a glow fills my belly.

"Other communities?" Miss Sullivan raises her hands like she's conducting an orchestra. "Yell them out!"

"Football team!"

"Old folk's home."

"Dolphins."

Miss Sullivan keeps her eyes closed and moves her arms and hands and it's like she's capturing the ideas like fireflies. "Communities are everywhere. In the ocean, in the air. Under the soil. Everywhere. People and animals and insects. Everywhere."

"Pigs," Macon yells. I stare at her in disbelief. She's so tall, even sitting down she towers over every other kid. Why is she saying that? It's my first time at school, and even I know she's asking for it.

Will snorts like a pig, chants under his breath, "Macon, bacon. Macon, bacon." His posse joins in.

Macon cries, "Pigs are some of the smartest most loving animals on the planet! Sows sing to their babies!"

Miss Sullivan tries to get some order back in the room. But the boys are riding a wave now, and the wave washes over the classroom and I feel it threatening to drown me.

Beep.

Fog.

Chapter 22

In the dream, I'm flying over the tops of the forest in a cape. It's night and clear and the floppy tops of the old trees glow silver from the moon. I dive into the forest, and whip around branches and dive through moss and float over mushrooms and say, "Hi." I swoop back up, and there's Blue in the distance, taller than the rest and I fly up, and it's a whole other world up here at the top of her canopy, and I land on one of the branches, and perch there.

I wake up sprawled between two of Blue's huge roots, my bottom soaked by the wet ground. It was a good dream.

Welcome home, Blue says.

"Oh, Blue." I stand, lean against her, and spread my arms against the scarves tied around her trunk. I tell her about Miss Sullivan, everything, the way she looks, and how she walks and about activism and action and community and how she's going to save the forest.

I like that Miss Sullivan, Blue says.

"Me too!" I say. "I knew you would!"

I do a twirl in front of Blue because I like the way my flowered skirt lifts up when I spin.

Talk to the trees, child. They need to know what's happening. Get to know them. Prepare them.

"I can only talk to you," I lie, because every day now I hear them humming and singing and sometimes whispering. I don't want to get to know them. Get to know them and then watch them die? I can't. I won't. I plop between Blue's roots. The fog rolls over my brain. I just want to go to sleep. And dream. Can I just lie down and dream? Good dreams?

Child, listen to me, Blue says, her voice insistent.

"Just let me sleep. I just need to sleep."

Blue is quiet for a while, but there's a buzzing I can feel, like she's thinking.

I'm glad you're here, Blue says, and it's in a different tone, a different energy. It wakes me up. It's the way she says the word "here", like it's loaded with energy.

This is the way Blue talks sometimes, saying things that make sense on a million different levels. I don't know if Blue's saying:

I'm glad you're here*, please don't go back into the fog.*

I'm glad you're here*, home with me now after such a hard time at school.*

I'm glad you're here *in this place in your life.*

I'm glad you're here *on the planet.*

Or all of the above.

Something about it makes me wake up completely. That's when I hear it. The whispering of the other trees becomes louder now. Like Blue is calling to them, and they're answering. Like they want me to hear them all loud and clear. It makes me want to cry. It scares me. I fish out my ear pods, stick them in my ears, and turn up the volume on a Big Leaf Maple. Yeah, I'd rather listen to a song of a tree than the actual tree. I know. I know.

OK, Blue, I'll listen, but only ones I don't know, only ones that come through headphones, only ones where I can turn down the volume when I want to.

***

Later, I go to the house. Mom's door is still closed. Apollo lays on the floor just outside her door.

I let Apollo out into the backyard, prepare his food. Twister rubs against my leg, and I feed her too. I look around and realize because of the fog, I haven't been doing the chores. The place is a pigsty. I get out the vacuum and clean the living room. I do the dishes, sweep the floor, take out the overflowing trash. I make two peanut butter and jelly sandwiches for dinner. I take one to Mom.

So much can go wrong when you're not paying attention.

My phone dings. "Hey kid, this is the third msg I've sent. Constance told me your Ma's doing better, but she isn't replying either. What's going on there? Msg me back. I mean it."

I put my phone on silent, and sit by the window with the binoculars.

Chapter 23

The snake's name is Belvedere. Besides Belvedere in his glass aquarium, the walls are covered with cobras, anacondas, and pythons.

This is Mr. Altishin's classroom. Apparently, he *really* loves snakes.

I'm awake more now in all of my classes. It's been a couple of weeks. I think it's because I'm getting used to school, or it's the tips and tricks, or it's Miss Sullivan, or it's Blue, or maybe all of the above.

We're reading out loud in class from a novel. Mr. Altishin likes to read to the snake. It makes the kids giggle. Someone will be reading out loud and he'll jump in and take over. He walks to the snake aquarium and reads the passage to Belvedere, who slithers and writhes and seems to like it. The other kids make faces, but I get it. Mr. Altishin gets it. Snakes are people, too.

He asks a student to continue reading, and it's a boy with poetry in him. I'm lulled into the beauty of this kid's soul and the beauty of the language. I love books. The way you can fall into them, and how safe it is inside.

I'm watching Belvedere to see which parts of which books he likes. At one point, Belvedere starts going berserk, twisting and shaking. I know it's not the novel. I know something is up.

Within seconds, the ground starts to shake. Markers fall from the whiteboard and pens roll from desks and Belvedere flip flops in his glass house.

"Earthquake!" I yell and jump beneath my desk, hands covering my head as ceiling tiles rain down.

I have my hands over my head and I can't hear anything, but then I start to hear giggling. Giggling? Then laughter.

Then Will yelling, "What's Clown Girl doing under her desk?"

Then Mr. Altishin is standing by my desk.

I crawl out. Will runs, arms flailing, falling on kids in desks, yelling, "Earthquake! Earthquake!"

"Miss LaForet, I think you best go speak with the nurse."

I want to blend into the walls, become a drawing of a snake, and disappear with the other drawings. I want to fall into the book we're reading and never come out again.

The nurse takes my temperature. She asks me what happened, but I don't tell her. I sit and wait for the teacher to come tell her but he doesn't, or for them to call my mother and she doesn't answer. This is what scares me the most, that Mom won't answer and the consequences, my own personal earthquake.

But she doesn't come. Instead, the nurse asks if I want her to call her, and I say as normally as possible, "No." And 20 minutes later when the bell rings between classes, she lets me go.

I walk the halls and four or five people call me Clown Girl. The name didn't catch on before, but after the earthquake fiasco, now it's everywhere. It doesn't help that today I have on a neon pink and green striped dress with neon red boots, and a long blue scarf. Will sees me and pinwheels against the lockers yelling "Earthquake," while his posse laughs. I put my head down and rush by.

After school, I'm with Blue but she's no help at all, telling me not to worry, to just to be myself.

I run up to mom's shed and open the big book of "Tips and Tricks". I try to find something about having visions. There's nothing. All I find are some "protection visualizations" in an appendix at the back. I try a few, but the book says it can take three months to see a difference. I yell, "I don't have that long!"

That night I have crazy dreams, not vision dreams, but mixed-up crazy ones.

I dream I'm a tree in the forest, one of the ones deep inside with moss dripping from its arms. I recognize the other trees as Mom and Aunt Angel and Macon and JAX. I dream that the loggers come and their cutting them down, cutting down the people I love, and soon I'll be next. My insides shiver with the sound of the saws, with my people falling around me.

Then the dream changes and an earthquake hits, and I'm still a tree, and we're all swaying and bending and some of us are uprooting and breaking and dying. And then it happens to me, I'm falling sideways, and my roots are yanking up.

I wake up in a cold sweat.

I have the dream over and over during the weekend, just in different order, but always the same with me being sawed down or uprooted.

I can't take it.

I can't go to school like this. I'll never survive.

Something has to change.

By Sunday night, I have the answer.

BLUE

Chapter 24

The child is offered to you. We give her to you. Her task is to create a bridge from we to you. She is bringing you back to us... if she can enter your world and not forget who she is.

She'd rather stay in the "we". We'd rather she stay, too. But many are born like her now, who have agreed to this sacrifice. It is not an easy bridge to build, not an easy task guiding souls back when many no longer even remember our language.

You separate yourself from us. How frightening to live on the outside, to exist on the edge, to always be on the verge of falling.

You think it is just you, isolated from us and from each other. *Oh, I am depressed*, you say, or *Oh I am sad* or *Oh I am anxious*. You say, *"I" can fix this. I can do it. Me. Me. Me.* But "you" can't fix it. You alone cannot. We can.

You've forgotten how to come to us for wisdom. You chop us down and let us burn and yet, you do not connect the dots.

If you think we are separate from you, and less than you, of course it is easy to spill your pollution, to chop us down. If you think we're separate and lower, how easy it is to think other humans are separate and lower, how easy it is to divide among yourselves, to mock and burn and chop each other. How easy it is then for the individual to divide inside themselves. For brain and heart to become strangers to each other.

How easy.

How dire.

Here in the forest, we do not weed each other out. We do not say, *Oh they are old, they go over here. They are broken, they go over there. They are different, they can't be with us.* There is no older or different, there is just "us".

We weave our stories together, root and fern and wing and weed. We are all embedded in a tapestry bound tight like a net.

You think *"I" must make my mark; "I" must succeed, "I" must show them how great I am*. It is difficult and exhausting. When you cross the bridge back to us, we can make our mark and be great—together. It will be easy and joyous.

I promise.

When the wind moves our branches, the spirit of our ancestors speak. Some hear our voices. We are calling you home. But many have tuned their ears away from the music. We have become mute to you.

When you do hear us speak you think you're going mad.

Follow the voice. It will take you to a gate. The gate has grown over with weeds and thorns. You may feel too tired to hack your way through. *What will I get out of all of the work to get to this gate? Success? Glory? Acknowledgment?*

No none of these.

You will get "we".

In the forest, we have this saying;

"Many are called.

But few choose."

MAISIE-GRACE

Chapter 25

I'm in front of the full-length mirror. The jeans are so tight. They're faded with a pre-made hole at the right knee. I wiggle and yank at the denim. What did Suzie, the clerk, call them? "Distressed?" Distressed is one thousand percent the right word.

I jerk and twist my legs trying to find some room.

If they cut the forest down with no thought at all, and if you feel you *are* the forest, then why wouldn't they cut you down.

If you act like yourself and everybody mocks you, then what's the use of being yourself?

If people think you're a clown, will anyone listen to you at all?

I zip and unzip the hoodie over my crop top. "Positive vibes," the hoodie says on one side. "High fives," on the other.

Hair tied back, high top tennis shoes on. I lean my face inches from the mirror. "The girls are going to be so jelly," I say.

"Normal," I whisper, making fists. "Normal."

"You're going to be *normal*," I demand of the girl in the mirror.

***

At first, normal doesn't seem so hard when I get to school. It seems easy in a fog, sitting at a desk, raising your hand, saying what they want to hear.

Smiling.

Nodding.

I'm learning so much. How to be quiet. How to sit still. How to speak only when spoken to. How to take a test. I already learned a long time ago how to keep my mouth shut about what I see – but this is a whole new level of learning.

I'm learning the other kids don't seem to know much. Maybe they know what's in the book we're reading for class (or maybe not), maybe they know what's on their phones, but they don't know the names of the trees that grow at the edge of the yard at recess or the ways of the birds or anything about bugs or the uses of the plants. They don't know about the earth right outside the door!

In English, Will checks out my new look. "The clown's new clothes," he yells for all to hear. Everyone laughs.

They'll see. Step by step. Slowly. I'll wear my new clothes, and keep my mouth shut, and sit still, and fit in. Soon I'll be *so* normal, no one will notice me at all. Soon, I'll be so normal, I'll be invisible.

Something is causing a ruckus over by the window. The whole class looks. It's the snake. It's going crazy, flipping and flopping. Just like before. I go rigid. I don't move. I don't know what's real.

Everything flows in slow motion—kids running and teachers shouting and announcements coming over the intercom. I don't trust what I'm seeing or hearing or feeling, so I sit. It's Macon who tackles me and throws me beside JAX's chair and covers us both with her body as ceiling tiles rain down.

It's not a big quake. Nobody gets hurt except a kid who bruises their leg when it gets caught in a bleacher in Gym.

Afterward, everyone is looking at me. Everyone is staring. They're making faces...faces like my mom made when I was 8.

You'd think that having a vision and being right would make you popular.

Ha ha ha ha ha.

Rumors spread like wildfire through the school.

That's the kid who predicted the earthquake. Where? Over there. She was homeschooled.

Weird.

Crazy.

Freak.

Cringe.

Everybody comes to know who I am. Heads turn and the whispers feel like shouts. Kids make a great show of veering around me in the hallway. Even some of the teachers act scared of me. I see JAX staring at me and catch her eye, and there's something there, something like connection. For a split second, I think, *There's my friend. She's still in there.* But then it's gone, and she turns her wheelchair and rolls back down the hall.

Macon sticks like glue. She uses her body to block some of the kids who are being particularly mean. She isn't helping. She thinks she's blocking but because she's so big and I'm so small, we're like some kind of Big Top show, some kind of sideshow freaks.

How am I going to ever fit in now? How can I get them to stop staring? I wrack my brains all week. On Thursday night, I stand in front of the bathroom room and stare myself down. I'm so sick of being different. I'm so sick of being me. I'm sick of the freckles. I'm sick of my nose and push it back until I look like a pig.

I mess up my hair until it really sticks out, a frizzy halo around my head. I'm sick of my clown hair.

I get Mom's scissors from the sewing kit. Back in the bathroom, I stretch out a strand of hair and hack it off. Something releases. Some relief happens. I hack off a second strand. A third. I go into a frenzy, cutting it within two inches of my scalp.

I stare at myself afterward, piles of red curls at my feet. My hair is curled up tight against my head. My eyes are so green and so big and take up my whole face. How is my skin so pale? Why are my eyes like that? I look in the mirror and don't think this has helped at all. I feel exposed. I feel seen.

I want to hide.

***

Friday after school I get Macon to go with me to the mall. We take a city bus. I remember back to school bootcamp with Aunt Angel, and how that seems like a lifetime ago. I'm surprised when the bus doesn't overwhelm me. *Well, maybe something is working*, I think.

When Macon and I walk into the store, Suzie is there. "I knew you'd be back," she says and laughs. She pulls out a short curl at my forehead. "So adorable! You're even cuter with short hair. I hate you."

She turns to Macon. "Aren't you a tall drink of water wrapped in overalls? Ooh, am I going to have fun dressing you!"

I'm about to tell her we're just here for me, that I want the most normal clothes she can find, when I see Macon's face, and don't say a word.

Suzie piles the dressing room with blacks and browns and greys for me first, while Macon waits. There's a hoodie this time with a different message. When I zip it up in front of the mirror, it says:

"Fun Fact," on my right side.

"I don't care," on my left.

Black skin-tight pants, crop tops, short jackets. I try it all on. I come out in a black outfit—black jacket, black crop top, black jeans, black boots.

Macon screams, "You look so sophisticated."

Suzie pumps up both palms toward the ceiling. "Vibes, baby," she says.

I'm over at a makeup counter picking out the most normal foundation and blush and mascara and nail polish I can find, when Macon comes out of the dressing room in clothes Suzie found for her.

Her transformation causes me to yelp. I shouldn't be surprised. I already saw she was beautiful at the bus stop that first day of school. Still, she looks like a goddess. It's just a striped jersey dress with a jacket and ankle boots, but she looks like a model, curvy and round and sexy and grown up.

"Hubba, hubba," Suzie says.

Macon turns beet red. She turns in front of the mirror, and I see she's crying but trying not to show it. Before I can get to her, she runs back into the dressing room. When she comes out, I ask her where her stuff is. She's empty handed.

"Oh, it's OK. I have no money. No way my parents would ever let me wear something like that."

I look at her and feel her sadness until her grief becomes mine and she must see it on my face, because she grabs my arm and gushes, "It was so much fun to dress up, though. Thank you. I loved it."

I pick her hand off my arm, move past her, and go to the dressing room. A clerk is loading up the dress and the rest of her outfit to return it to the shelf. I take the outfit from her, come out, and put it in my cart.

Macon protests. "Oh no, Maisie, no. I don't have anywhere to wear it anyway. My parents will kill me."

I pull out a credit card. It's my mother's. "I'm paying for all of it." Macon looks at the card, and makes an oh-no-you're-going-to-get-into-so-much-trouble face. "Oh, don't worry," I say, handing the card to Suzie who takes it without question. "She owes me."

I watch Suzie ring it all up. Kaching. The whole frickin' world owes me. Kaching. Owes me for making me a freak of nature to begin with. Kaching. Owes me for making me have to go to school. Kaching. Owes me for the logging. Kaching. Owes me for whatever this crap is I'm supposed to be doing to make a difference.

Owes me for EVERYTHING!

Kaching.

Kaching.

Kaching.

Chapter 26

Miss Sullivan is holding a baseball cap upside down in her palm.

"Your midterm is an oral report and it's going to be a group project," she says, lightly bouncing the hat in her palm and walking between the rows. "You're going work with in groups of threes. This hat," she holds it up, "contains a bunch of numbers. You'll pick one and find the other two classmates with the same number."

I'm sitting in the first desk near the door and she starts with me. I put my hand in and come out with the number five.

After everyone has chosen, kids run around trying to find their matches. Macon is at my desk. She shows me her slip of paper. It's number two.

"Oh shoot," she says, "I want to be in your group." Just then, Will sidles in fast and grabs the paper out of her hand and throws his at her.

She bends to pick it up. "Five!" she cries and hugs me.

"Dodged that bullet," I hear Will tell his friends.

Macon turns to the rest of the class and screams, "Five! Anyone else have a five!" and I can see JAX noticing and looking at her number and then turning to kids around her trying to swap.

"All right, no swapping numbers!" Miss Sullivan says because every kid is doing it now. "When you find your partners," Miss Sullivan has to yell because of the pandemonium, "put your desks together and make a group! Hurry up. We don't have a lot of time."

Macon pushes a desk next to mine and sits openly smiling at me.

"Jaqueline Watanabe!" Miss Sullivan says. "What number do you have?"

I turn to look at JAX. She sighs an exaggerated sigh, scowls and moves her chair. She comes up to Macon and me. She flips the piece of paper onto my desk like she's tossing a cigarette butt.

Number five.

Macon yells, "Yay, JAX!" while I fall down inside my turtleneck and wish I could disappear.

JAX and Macon – two of the biggest outsiders at the whole school! Why can't I be with a normal group, like Lisa Michael and her happy little trio? I stare at Lisa wistfully, look back at JAX and Macon. Macon's hair is all over the place and she's back in her overalls and showing too much of her gums as she smiles. JAX has a temporary tattoo on her face of a skull.

"Oh," Macon says, and throws both of her arms up, "I get to be with the two coolest people in class."

I shake my head.

Miss Sullivan is talking. "...no more than five minutes picking out the community you want to focus on. You can only choose one. Here's the important part. I want you to pick a *local* community. No polar bears or penguins or camels... focus on Lester County and this wonderful state of Oregon."

Blue told me to always look for the light, and Miss Sullivan is like a glaring spotlight. "You'll be giving a report in front of the class, so make sure *you* find it interesting. If it's not interesting to you, it won't be interesting to anyone!"

Energy travels up my body. This is it. I can feel it. I turn to JAX and Macon. "Forests," I whisper. I meant to yell it but that thing is caught in my throat.

"Pigs!" Macon yells.

"Yeah, do not care." JAX scowls.

"Forests," I whisper again, louder. "Forests, Macon, please."

"Pigs!" Macon calls louder, smiling at me like this is a game.

"Please, Macon, please! Forests."

Macon blushes. "OK! Forests. Sure, of course, Maisie-Grace. Forests! Absolutely."

JAX says nothing. She's opened a notebook and is sketching and ignoring us.

After five minutes, Miss Sullivan has everyone call out their communities.

High school football team.

Animal shelter.

Church.

School band.

Deer hunters.

Fishermen.

Butterflies.

"This very weekend," Miss Sullivan says. "I want you to get together and visit your community if that's possible." She hands one of the kids a stack of papers, and we pass them from table to table. "Give your parents this form that explains what we're asking because some of you will need help getting to your destinations. If you can't visit your community in person, do it all online. But, please please try to do it in person!"

She goes on, "This will be a multi-media presentation. Besides the facts and the report, we want images. We want music. We want slideshows. Add some dancing if you feel like it. Dress up!

"For today, each of you will choose a role that you're going to play in the oral report. Someone will be in charge of the factual research, someone will do images, and someone else will do the writing."

"Research!" Macon yells too loud before Miss Sullivan stops speaking. All heads turn toward us.

"Oink," Will yells. "Snort. Snort. Snort."

"Will! Control yourself," Miss Sullivan says. "Now let's get started. I'll be walking around checking on your progress."

Macon is holding up her hand to JAX and me like we're her teachers.

"Yes Macon, you can do the research," I say.

"Illustrations," JAX says, not looking up.

"I'll do the writing then," I say.

Macon starts talking about coming to my house after school to go in person to the woods.

I say, "What if we camp out?"

"Yes!" Macon screams and turns to JAX, and Macon's face falls. "Oh, sorry. Sorry. I can get my mom to help you, JAX, if it's too hard to get a wheelchair in the woods..."

"I don't need help!" JAX hisses. "I'm perfectly capable of getting there."

"Fun!" Macon yells, clapping. She raises her hand toward JAX and me.

"You don't need to raise your hand, Macon," JAX says.

"No, I'm high-fiving," she says. "Come on," she cries, pumping her palms toward us. "Come on!"

I high five her and she smacks my palm so hard it stings. She doesn't know her own strength. JAX ignores her and goes back to drawing.

Chapter 27

The day of the camping, I'm down in the clearing next to Blue setting things up. Tent, fire pit, a table for food. I'm nervous, and it's not about the camping. Every day the waiting gets worse. Every day, I pace and fret. It's been weeks and the loggers haven't shown up.

Come!

Just come!

Get it over with already!

***

Macon did research and found a forestry expert and she's showing up today to talk to us. I'm adjusting Blue's ribbon waiting for JAX and Macon when the forester appears at the top of the path. She's got the light. She walks down the logging road surrounded by a glow.

"Miss Bartholomew," she says. "Call me Miss B." She shakes my hand. She's tall and has a brown ponytail down her back, wiry muscles in her arms and calves, a face that's soft and older than Mom's, and green eyes that float. She says, "I certainly don't get this opportunity often, to come out to a local forest and talk to young women about my favorite subject in the whole world."

I go and fuss with the tent, and re-arrange the chairs, and make sure the food table is right. I'm too shy or too scared to talk to her.

JAX rolls down the path. She's in a different chair, with fat tires like a mountain bike, and she maneuvers it like an athlete.

"Nice wheels!" Miss B calls up to her.

"All-terrain," JAX beams. "Dad got it for me for my last birthday. My first time using it." Her phone bings, and she looks annoyed and types a text. It bings again a minute later, and I know it's her dad checking up on her. She turns the phone off and tosses it in her backpack.

Macon lopes down the path with her sleeping bag and backpack, a dog at her side. Apollo trots up and the dogs flop over each other.

I introduce JAX and Macon to Miss B. I introduce Apollo to Macon's dog, a sheepdog with long fur. "That's Olaf," Macon says. I grab Macon's sleeping bag and put it in the tent. JAX has a big pack attached to the back of her chair but I'm too scared to offer to help.

"Well girls," Miss B says, "We'd better get started before it gets dark. Then I'll leave you to your camping."

We stand at the edge of the forest. It's dark and cold and wet. An owl hoots. It's that time of day when everything settles into a deep peace.

"Before I do anything else, I just like to *feel* the forest, first," Miss B says, closing her eyes and putting her head back like she's smelling the air. "Can you feel it?"

Macon and JAX put their heads back and close their eyes. I watch Miss B.

"Every forest has a different feel," she says. "Every tree is different, true, but every forest is unique as a whole."

I've never met anyone else like me before, someone else who feels the forest.

"Do you know how many cultures have trees as core to their mythology?" she asks. For the first time, I notice her walking stick. It has symbols burned into it.

"Trees that talk."

"Wishing trees."

"Trees as oracles."

"Adam and Eve's tree."

"Buddha's Bodhi tree."

"Pagan sacred groves."

"Have you seen pictures of the World Tree?" She lifts the stick toward the canopy like she's commanding an orchestra. "Branches holding up the heavens." She moves the stick down. "Trunk connecting the sky to the earth, roots burrowing to the underworld. It's all connected. Scientifically, yes, but it's connected in a metaphoric way."

She's quiet for a while, then tells us we can open our eyes.

"Do you know how many of my scientist coworkers make fun of me for 'feeling' the forest?" She walks up to Blue. "Scientists like to break everything into small parts and smaller parts and smaller parts. That's like taking off a finger and studying it without studying the whole arm, or studying an arm without studying the whole body. Or studying the whole body without looking at its environment." She pats Blue. "A forest is so much more than the sum of its parts, right old girl?

"I mean imagine just taking a piece of this big Doug Fir's bark, and slicing it a thousand times, and studying it under a microscope. Don't get me wrong, you'll find information that way, but it's so separate from the whole.

"This mother tree here," she says, looking up at Blue. "She's probably 150 years old." I want to tell her that Blue isn't necessarily a female, but I don't. I want to tell her that Blue is a "they" not a "she".

"Imagine how much she's *seen*. People were just coming over the Oregon Trail. When she was growing up, this forest would've been jam-packed with trees five stories high. Trees so high that at the top of them entire ecosystems were growing in the branches. Imagine the moss, the animals, how primitive and wild and *abundant* it was."

It feels like Miss B is singing. I can see the old forest from over a hundred years ago, and I can hear it. A song, a chorus, a gospel. Not just these trees in front of me, but the past trees, the ancestor trees.

The others.

"Macon told me about the logging," Miss B. says. She takes a moment to look at each of us, one by one. "I'm so sorry." She's so sincere, I feel like crying.

She adds in a whisper. "Sometimes I think all of this analysis and parsing things into tiny parts is just ruining our ability to imagine." She shakes her head. "Like when we cut trees down, we're losing a part of our imagination."

I stare at her. How did Macon find her? She's a miracle wrapped in cargo pants. I look at Macon like I've never seen her before.

"OK, for the science now," she says. "Believe me, I'm not against the science. It's just not the *only* thing." Macon takes out a notebook and pen, and I wished she was taking notes from the beginning. I worry that she didn't write down the magic part. Why isn't anyone writing about the magic?

Miss B. rests the stick against Blue and holds up her right hand. "This is the spirit of the forest." Next, she holds up her left hand. "This is the science."

Her palms face each other and she intertwines her fingers like she's holding her own hand. "This is the spirit married to the science." She unlocks her fingers and raises her right hand, "But with just the science, the left hand doesn't know what the right hand knows and vice versa."

We walk into the forest. JAX's chair cannot manage the forest floor, so she stays back and sketches. As Miss B. walks, she leans and picks up forest debris and stuffs it in the tiny pockets in her cargo pants and vest. A cone at her thigh, a twig with needles at her upper arm, a bit of bark in her back pocket. I get an image of a squirrel and a Christmas calendar, climbing up and opening her pockets one by one, finding bits of forest fun.

"When we think of old growth," Miss B says, motioning around her, "sometimes we just think of one tree. We think: this is an old growth tree, that is an old growth tree. But really old growth means a whole system of plants and animals acting as a network."

"So, when you're talking in class about 'community', this is a truly diverse and interconnected community, the very essence of the word."

"Miss B," I say, "I heard something about how trees communicate. They communicate right?"

"That is such a great question," she says. "Just below our feet, the tree root hairs work with the threads of the mushroom roots and form a network of communication, a 'wood-wide web'."

We walk deeper into the cold dark forest. "Moving into the forest is moving backward in time." She takes off her backpack, reaches in, and pulls out worn blocks with words on them. She put the blocks by the trees and bushes.

"Deer fern."

"Sword fern."

"Wood fern."

"Red huckleberry."

"Cascade Oregon-grape."

Macon stops to write them down.

"I'll come back later and pick these up – there's no rush," Miss B says. "We can name all of these plants and trees, but I wouldn't say that we truly know them. No scientist anywhere knows *everything* about *any* forest. There's so much we still don't know."

"Doug Fir."

"Western Hemlock."

"Western Red Cedar."

"Pacific Yew."

Macon interrupts breathlessly, pencil still making notes. "What happens to the animals when the trees are cut down?"

Miss B squats to examine some mushrooms. "Squirrels and martens and bears are going to go looking for another old growth habitat. We're lucky here, because they can go to the county park just over the valley there. Although if enough people cut down their forests around here that ecosystem will fill up really fast. At least for now, the animals here are pretty lucky."

Miss B tells us more, about moss and bark, nest and burrow, until the sun goes down and the forest grows so dark we can't see.

"Let's head out," she says. We walk out and JAX ignores us, head down over her sketchbook, drawing like a girl possessed.

We come back to Blue. There's a sapling growing next to Blue that I hadn't noticed before.

Miss B examines it like it's a precious gem. "Saplings don't have the light to photosynthesize, and a tree like this one pumps the younger one's roots full of sugar using the wood wide web."

"This queen here," Miss B says, rubbing her hand down Blue's moss, like she's petting Blue's hair. "She has the deepest roots, the most fungal connections, and she's sending the most nutrients to the saplings. She's the Tree of Life." She adjusts Blue's scarves. I tell her why the scarves are there, and how Blue will be saved, but the rest of the forest is going to be logged, and she leans in and whispers to Blue's bark, "Sorry!" and I nearly start crying again.

"Well, it's getting dark," she says. "I need to let you girls get on with your camping."

She turns to us with sad eyes. "I'm so sorry about the logging, girls. I really am. I've been in love with forests and have watched them burn to the ground, and I've witnessed the clearcutting and it's broken my heart. Over and over. But you've got to love, even if it breaks your heart."

"What can we do to stop it?" I say and it comes out like a croak.

Miss B picks up soil near Blue's roots and rubs it between her fingers. I reach down and do the same.

"Soil is the decomposition of all of the creatures and the shedding of the trees. It's so rich," Miss B says. "At first, scientists thought soil was just dirt, but then they studied it and the forest started talking to them."

I laugh. It comes out as a bark. She's talking about forests talking and I'm kind of losing it.

"What you can do is what you're doing. You're paying attention. You're asking for information. You're talking about it."

She's rubbing her palm up and down Blue now, and Blue purrs.

"Did you know that when a tree is cut," Miss B says, "it sends electrical signals like wounded human tissue?"

I almost scream out. *No. No, no, no, no, no.*

Don't tell me that.

No!

MACON

Chapter 28

Omygosh, Miss B is leaving and I want to grab her and hug her but I just put out my hand, and she shakes it, like we're grownups, and I'm blushing down to my toes. I've been living around these trees my whole life and didn't know anything. It's like I was totally blind.

And after she leaves, I run up to JAX but she's sketching like crazy and I run up to Maisie-Grace but she's kind of lost, but that's OK because what just happened? What just happened?

Can I find someone who talks to pigs? That's what I want to be when I grow up, someone who knows about animals like Miss B. knows about trees. Where are the people who can talk to pigs? Who can feel pigs? Who knows their whole history? Could you imagine someone who had this way of talking about sows and weaners like they knew the pigs could talk and someone who would tell their stories like Miss B just did for the forest? And I think what is the mythology of pigs and think about all of the stories with pigs like The Three Little Pigs and Charlotte's Web and This Little Piggy Went to Market, but I want more.

More.

I'm trying to calm down but I can't, and now we're at the food table and it glows in the dark because Maisie-Grace has hung lanterns in branches. All the food is so colorful, like an art project – pumpkin, lime, lemon, blueberry.

And Maisie-Grace names the dishes — lavender cake squares, avocado chocolate mousse, lettuce peanut-ginger wraps (I write it all down so I can remember) and the fruits and vegetables are glowing too, carrots and grapes and apples. Maisie says she spent all day cooking it and I imagine the kitchen where the aroma is fruity and nobody is frying pork.

I brought three pears I picked off our tree and I get them from my pack and give them to Maisie-Grace and she puts them in the center of the table and says one of the pears is me, and one is her, and one is JAX. She calls them "Pear goddesses", and I'm so happy, so very very happy that my pears are goddesses.

And we eat, and I'm waiting because I'm expecting we'll cook meat over the fire pit, but there's never any meat and in my whole life I've never had a meal without meat, and I think this is what it means to be a hippie, and I think, maybe I'm a hippie, ha ha, wouldn't Dad love that. Ha ha ha.

And JAX brings out these neon-colored balls for dessert that she calls *Dango* and they're Japanese and sweet and gooey and I've never had Japanese food before, ever. In one night, so many things I've never seen or eaten or known before. I know my house is just over the hill but it's like in a totally different universe.

But Maisie-Grace is still checked out, she's sort of smiling and nodding, like she used to do at school, and the sun is all the way down and the fire is so crackly, and the moon comes up over the hill and I feel like I've walked into a fairy tale, and it's such a good place and I can see why you'd want to never leave, ever.

And my mom gave me stuff to make s'mores, but Maisie has her own marshmallows and chocolate, and we roast her marshmallows. "These are vegan," she says. Apparently, my marshmallows have animal proteins in them, and her chocolate is vegan too, and I eat the s'mores and they're so delicious, and I'm thinking, Am I vegan now?

JAX won't show us the sketches, and at first, she's all moody and dark, but the owls start hooting and the moon turns the trees silver and the fire makes everybody's face glow and JAX glances up and smiles, and sometimes even looks at Maisie-Grace in a nice way, although Maisie doesn't notice.

The moon comes up, full now, and Maisie-Grace seems to "wake up" from her trance, and in a soft voice, she starts naming all of the moons for the whole year and soon she's up twirling and naming them in front of the fire.

"Harvest moon." Twirl.

"Sap moon." Twirl.

"Blue moon." Twirl.

"Corn moon." Twirl.

"Hunter moon."

"Frosty moon."

"Dying grass moon."

"Beaver moon."

"Strawberry moon."

Twirl.

Twirl.

Twirl.

"This could take a while," JAX says, and rolls her eyes so hard I think they'll pop out but then she smiles and it's so nice to see JAX sort of happy.

And then Maisie-Grace says the funniest things, she says she talks to trees and she has always talked to the big tree with the scarves and how her name is Blue and Blue talks back to her. And I want to ask her about the earthquake, because everybody at school knows she predicted it, but every time you bring it up, she shrinks so I don't say anything. But I do ask about the scarves and she says because the loggers are coming, the scarves are there to save Blue.

And then it's time to go to bed, or go to the tent, and I set up JAX's sleeping bag, and I pick up JAX and her legs are so skinny and she's so fierce you wouldn't think she'd be so light and I put her in the tent, and kneel there holding the soles of her feet and she can't feel it but she doesn't stop me.

And we all pile into the tent with me in the middle and I want to cry because this is what it must feel like to have sisters.

JAX

Chapter 29

The ceiling is freakin' confusing. Where am I? It's not white, not plaster. It's blue and vinyl. I blink and blink and it takes forever to understand that I'm not at home. I'm in a tent staring at nylon. But what's even weirder is who's flying across the "ceiling" today.

Me! I'm the superhero! I've never seen myself before. Ever. I'm not sure I like it because my stupid cape is stuck in the freakin' wheels of my chair. It's a red cape and I'm seeing the visual of myself above me yanking it, but it won't frickin' *budge*.

The image annoys the crap out of me.

I hear a noise at my feet and prop up on my elbows.

Macon's on her belly looking out the flap. MG is nowhere.

"What the hell are you doing?"

"Shhhhhh!" she whispers so loudly it could wake my dad a mile away. "Maisie-Grace is talking to Blue!"

"Fascinating," I say, rolling my eyes.

"Shhhh! Let me listen," she says, waving me away.

I braid my hair and get Macon to stop eavesdropping and get me into my chair. It's been a long time since I haven't gotten myself into my chair and I want to snap at Macon just because I can't stand someone carrying me like I'm a baby.

When we roll up, MG comes up to me, holding something out. "You left this out last night."

My sketchbook! I snatch it out of her hands. It's open to the rough sketch I did of her around the fire last night. I do not like her seeing that I'm sketching her. "What are you doing going through my stuff?"

"It was open to that page. The wind was blowing it. Blue told me to look."

"What else did Blue tell you, Maisie-Grace?" Macon asks, running to the cooler and handing us water bottles and pears, trying to broker peace with fruit.

"Maybe Blue wants you to go through my whole backpack," I say, scowling.

MG's face flares red. "For your information, I'd rather not even know how to talk to trees. I'd rather not be this person who sees everything all the time!"

"Poor widdle MG," I say, and she looks like she's been slapped, and I feel sorry for her for a second. Last night when the moon was up and the forest behind us –it was the first time I've felt good in a long time. I don't know why this is upsetting me. Or is it the image of me with a stuck cape? For some reason, I'm so annoyed and sick of everyone and everything.

MG bends and screams in my face. "Well for your information, Blue told me that all three of us should tell our problems to them!"

I back my chair up. "What are you talking about?"

"They told me that we're all in pain and if we scream, they can take it!" MG screams.

I roll my eyes.

"That's what they said! It is!" MG yells, tears coming into her eyes. "They said that we can't do anything to help the forest when we're all so messed up, and 'out of alignment' (she uses air quotes), and we need to get back into our happy selves and try to get rid of all the heavy stuff on top."

"Tell our problems to Blue?" Macon asks. "What does that mean?"

"That's all I know. It's not complicated," MG says.

"Isn't that like pollution? Emotional pollution?" Macon asks. "Like won't it be toxic for her...ummm, I mean them?"

"They say they can transform it," MG says.

"Whatever," I say. "You guys do what you want. Don't expect me to do something so stupid."

"It's not stupid," MG says, face big and red like a balloon.

"It's OK, Maisie. I'll do it. I'll do it," Macon says, running up to Blue. "Look, I'll go first." Macon puts one hand out to touch the bark and puts it back down. She leans, fidgets, turns, fidgets.

"Omygawd, just lean up against them. They won't bite," I yell.

She settles on standing sideways, leaning against the bark and the scarves, and whispers toward the trunk.

"Macon, you gotta speak up," I say, annoyed.

When Macon screams, it comes out like a hot wind shoving us backward into hell.

"I have a right to say no! You don't own me! You're not always right! I have a right to be me!" She falls to her knees, her forehead against Blue. MG runs up and puts a hand on her shoulder.

"I have rights," Macon whispers. "I do."

Macon and MG come back, Macon looking like she's been beaten.

I want out of here. I feel trapped. I want to pump the wheels of my chair up the hill and go home, but I can't. Maybe my cape is stuck. I can't flippin' move.

"OK, it's my turn," MG says. "I have a lot to yell!"

She goes up to Blue and puts her arms straight out, her hands in fists. "This forest is not for sale!"

"Louder!" Macon yells.

"*You can't put a price tag on everything and sell it! Not everything is for sale!*" MG screams at the top of her lungs.

"Go!" Macon cries.

"*I don't want the dreams! Why do I have to dream!*" She's almost hyperventilating now.

I don't want to feel for MG. I don't want to care. When she staggers back to us, I feel like vomiting. I want to leave, but when I pump the handles, instead of heading up the hill, my chair moves toward Blue. Macon runs up and maneuvers me between Blue's roots.

I lean and put my hand on the bark. There's something about the energy, like this big damn tree is reaching inside you and pulling it all out of you.

"Why didn't you tell me? How could you not tell me? What kind of friend does that?"

I pant with a hoarse voice. I feel so exhausted. So profoundly freakin' tired.

"Why? Why?" I scream, and the "why" is so much more. It's about everything, about my life, my mom, everything. The why is the question I ask myself every day.

"Why?" I scream, pounding the bark.

Exhausted, I raise my hand to signal Macon and she brings me back. Twister the cat comes and jumps in my lap. MG is slumped away from me. I can't see her face.

A loud grinding noise erupts at the top of the hill, engines revving.

We all jump.

"Oh no. No. No. No. No. No," MG screams, running in circles like she doesn't know what to do.

The engine roars again and MG runs up the hill with Macon after her, and me pumping the wheels to keep up. The dogs bark and run, Apollo trailing behind.

We crest the hill. A huge machine is moving toward us, blocking the path. We stop, dogs barking like crazy.

The driver sits high above us. He leans out.

"You kids cain't be in these woods. We're gonna be loggin' in here starting today. Go on, get your stuff and git on out."

Chapter 30

Sounds become the only thing that exist. Sounds become hail pounding on my head. Sounds become my life.

Chainsaws like thousands of bees. Buzzing. Screeching. Wood cracking, splintering, a pause, a whoosh, a speed. A thud like a mini earthquake, vibrations traveling up my legs. One thud, another, another.

And...the sudden surprising silence of the birds. The birds seem to have lost their voices.

I didn't expect to fall in love with them. The others. I didn't expect their humming and whispered words to enter my dreams until each one became like friends or family. I didn't expect my way of seeing to change when the logging started.

Paper isn't just paper anymore. The wooden kitchen table, the junk mail, my books, notebooks, textbooks. They aren't what they seem. They all used to be a forest.

And still outside, the daily thudding. Every time the earth moves, my body shakes and my stomach clenches.

***

Normal. I have to go to school. I have to cross the bridge. Breathe and visualize and name and count and breathe and visualize and name. And pretend. And nod.

Distressed jeans, and high tops, and blush, and eye shadow, and another new zip hoodie.

"Live your..."

Zip.

"Best life."

My phone dings. It's Aunt Angel. "Kid, this is the sixth text I've sent you. Call me. You told Constance your mom is better,

141

and I know she's not. I've been trying to get her for days and she's not picking up."

I don't reply. I don't need this now. I go into Mom's dark room, grab her phone. If I could text a message to Angel from her phone, she's leave me alone. But it's locked and I don't know the code.

I grab the uneaten sandwich off the bedstand and throw it into the overflowing sink.

I can't deal with *any* of this.

***

In the computer lab, we're doing research for our project. The kids are all in their groups at the computers, faces glowed up by the screens. It's eerily quiet after the noise at home. Macon whispers that she hears the trees falling up at her house.

"Are you OK? Is Blue OK?" she asks, and I smile and nod and try not to scream. JAX is hunched over drawing the forest in black ink. Macon goes on and on about our time camping and how horrible it is that they're just lopping the trees down like they're nothing, and how much she liked Miss B. She looks at me tears in her eyes and I have to set my jaw, hard.

Somebody drops a book and I jump. I jump too far and too high.

"Whoa," JAX says.

Macon just stares at me. I'm pretty sure she's about ready to kneel and hold the bottom of my feet.

"I have an idea," Macon says, and swivels back to the computer. She types into the search bar "gentler ways to log forests".

It's pretty much the same as holding my feet.

Lots of links pop up.

"New Forestry: A Kinder, Gentler Approach to Logging"

"Selective Logging."

"Sustainable Logging."

I push Macon out of the chair with my body, and click.

And click.

And click.

I print the articles.

Now it's my turn to have an idea.

"Can you write up the Miss B stuff, Macon?"

"I already have," she says.

"Can you email it to me?"

"Yes!" Macon almost yells.

"JAX, can you send me some of images? They don't have to be perfect."

"Why do you want them now? The report isn't due for like two weeks," she says, without looking up from her drawing.

"I just need them, OK?"

I turn back to the computer, google, "Alternatives to wood."

"Bamboo."

"Cork."

"Hemp."

"Repurposing plastic."

I print those too.

***

Meanwhile, something else is happening. I'm having visions. Day-time visions, but they're not about the future. They're about forests. Not dead trees, but alive old growth, more wild and more ancient than any forest I've ever seen. It's the vision that Miss B gave us, and now it's entered my soul.

I'm sitting at my desk, and roots swirl up from the floor and into my feet and wrap around my body, crawl up and become bark. It feels like a big hug. My arms become branches where moss starts to grow.

The hallway between classes sprouts vines and branches that swarm the walls and crawl across the ceiling. Kids arch and turn into trees or hunch and shrink into critters. Bark grows thick along a wall of lockers.

I'm walking from the school bus stop down to the house, ignoring the screeching saws, the way the earth shakes when a tree hits, ignoring, ignoring, and an acre of perfect old forest flies from the sky and lands at my feet. Trees, roots, and all. It's like an old growth stand from many hundreds of years ago. It's so thick, so healthy, it takes my breath away. I hear the words:

"Tree wisdom." It keeps repeating like a mantra. "Tree wisdom. Tree wisdom."

It's like the dying forest is crying out with the story of its ancestors.

JAX won't send the photos. I'm texting and she won't reply. I'm finished adding my info to Macon's, and everything is ready but the illustrations. I need the visuals. The art will make a huge difference.

I decide to go to her house. I haven't been to her house in years – except on the school bus – and the idea makes me shake.

I run through the woods, going the way we used to always go when we were little, when JAX and I were friends, when she could walk. The loggers aren't here today. They come or they don't come and there's no sense to it, so I never know when to be ready.

I haven't been down since it started. The forest is like a battle scene in a war, torn up earth and fallen trees and severed branches. It's like walking on top of the dead. It's like a monster reached down with a claw and tore up everything. There is nothing gentle about it. The branches of the still standing are torn off and smashed, jammed and broken. They've piled the downed trees to the side. I lose my breath and lean against Blue.

Child, speak to them. There isn't much time.

"Them? I am! I have!"

Speak to them!

"What do you want from me?" I scream. Already my heart is torn into bits. I run, ducking through the barbed wire fence that separates our land from Macon's, tearing my dress. I race along the creek, crawling under another barbed wire and down the dirt path that leads to JAX's house.

My phone dings, and it's Angel again, and I want to scream.

Chapter 31

JAX's cottage with its mossy roof, red door, and flaky shutters is like a fairy tale house full of legends, sadness, and secrets.

I knock and ring the doorbell but nobody answers. I try to get the mud off my hoodie and fix my hair and calm down.

It doesn't work. I get mad. Mad because she can't even do this one simple thing. Mad because monsters are eating the forest. Mad because the bridging and pretending is so freaking exhausting.

I text her. "At your house! Where are you? I need the illustrations." I add a prayer emoji, then delete it. I'm not going to beg.

My phone beeps. Finally.

"Hello. Who is this?"

"Oh, please, you know who it is. It's MG!"

"This is Jacqueline's father. Is this Maisie-Grace?"

"Oh, sorry Mr. W. I'm trying to talk to JAX about a class project!!"

"Jaqueline is just now coming out of her doctor's appointment. Please go inside the house and wait. We will be home soon. Do you remember the spare key?"

I do. Beneath the concrete gargoyle near the front step. I text: "I found it. TY. See you soon."

It's so weird going into their house, like meeting a friend you haven't seen for years. Everything is the same. They haven't changed a thing since the accident, since I was banished forever. The living room is dark and cool, with bookshelves to the ceiling on all of the walls. Red cracked sofa and chairs, the fireplace. I feel like my old self, standing there with the soft light hitting the oriental rug. Like I'm meeting myself again. Like when I lost JAX, I lost me.

Then I see a picture of JAX's mom and her eyes are following me around the living room, and I feel awful and judged and run back to JAX's room.

It's not safe in JAX's room either. I flashback to the last time I was there, the time when I lost my best friend forever.

***

It was after the accident. Mom and I were coming over every day. Some days I just sat by JAX's bed and cried the whole time. On this specific day, Mom was with JAX's dad in the kitchen heating up food. She'd bought art supplies for JAX, and I went into her room and put them by the side of the bed.

I'd also brought crossword puzzles. They were supposed to help JAX's brain. I sat by her bed and read the clues.

It must've been for really little kids because the clues were ridiculous. At one point, JAX grabbed it out of my hand and threw it across the room. She had bad days. Angry days. I didn't blame her.

Yeah, it wasn't *her* I blamed.

"I'm sorry," I cried, hands over my face.

"You're sorry. I'm the one who threw it," JAX said.

I cried harder.

JAX said, "Ugh, ever since the accident, it's like I gotta take care of all the sad people!"

I kept crying.

"MG, for crying out loud, it's not your fault."

"It is!"

I cried harder and harder, until I became hysterical, hiccupping and hyperventilating and having to put my head between my knees.

"What is going on?"

I spoke some garbled words toward the floor.

"What?" JAX whispered. She knew it was something big now, I could tell by the whisper. She reached out and took my hands off my face. "What?" This was so soft, but also scary, the way she said it.

I blurted out a full sentence. I blurted out a sentence to end all sentences. "I dreamt about the accident before it happened!" I went into hysterics again.

"What?"

"What?"

"What?"

JAX just kept repeating that one word, over and over. "What? What? What?"

I doubled over in the chair.

"Say it again!" I didn't answer. "Do it," she commanded.

"I dreamt about the accident the morning before it happened."

I saw JAX's face fall. I saw something in her die. I hated myself more than I already hated myself.

"You always tell me about your dreams. Why would you not tell me? I don't understand."

I kept crying.

She stared at me, eerily quiet and even-toned. "You could've saved my mom? I don't care about my legs, but you could've saved my mom?"

I couldn't look her in the eyes. I couldn't tell her why. I couldn't tell her that my mom had been freaking out about my dreams for a while by then, like really freaking out, like she was losing it. I couldn't tell her that after the dream about the accident, I'd told my mom, and she stared at me with such fear and dread, and it was like she didn't love me anymore. Like her heart was closing. I couldn't tell JAX that my mom grabbed my shoulders and made me promise not to tell JAX, and to never ever say anything about *any* dream ever again. How her fear leaped over and entered me. I couldn't tell JAX that the look in my mom's eyes made me feel so abandoned. I couldn't tell her that since that moment, I'd had so many dreams, and I'd never told anyone any of them. I couldn't even begin to tell JAX how horribly lonely that was.

"Unforgivable!" JAX screamed. "Unforgivable!" She swung her fists, hitting me on the arm.

"JAX. JAX. JAX." I was standing over her, trying to calm her down, or hug her, or change the past.

"Get out," she screamed. I fumbled to pick up the crossword puzzles. She slapped them out of my arms. "Never come back! Ever."

I ran past Mom in the hallway as she was carrying a bowl of cannelloni toward JAX's room. I ran out the door. I ran headlong to Blue.

***

Now, alone in JAX's room, the memory is more like it's happening all over again. I put in my earbuds to drown out the memories. On my phone, I choose the voice of a Weeping Willow.

Shhhhhh whoosh.

Shhhhhh whoosh.

Ding.

JAX has tacked up dozens of her black ink drawings. I can't find any of the forest, though. She must have her sketchpad with her.

I keep getting pulled toward her closet. It has two white slatted doors that are glowing. It's the light again, like the glow that surrounds Miss Sullivan or Miss B. The closet is screaming: "Go that direction! Look at me! Open me!"

My pulse is racing. I touch the knobs and they're vibrating.

Shhhhh whoosh.

Shhhh whoosh.

Ding.

When I open the doors, it's like a wave of water floods over me, but it's not water, it's color—lavender and lemon and lime and orange and every color of the rainbow in between.

Shhhhh whoosh.

Shhhhh whoosh.

Ding.

Dozens of paintings hang from the walls. JAX's clothes are gone and instead, there's a mini gallery. The paintings are nothing like her edgy inkwork. The lines are round and whimsical.

I see someone who looks like me. I go up to study it. Color sings from it. I'm flying through the night sky wearing a cape made of the forest. It's unbelievably beautiful. It's like one of my dreams. My good dreams. Just staring at the painting makes me feel a love for myself that brings tears to my eyes. It's like my mother's shed, but different.

I see Macon and laugh. She's on a bicycle with wings, a pig as her wingman.

There are a lot of kids from school here, all superheroes flying, over forests and cemeteries and cars and cities.

Shhhh whoosh.

Shhhh whoosh.

Ding.

Miss Sullivan, too. She's an African Goddess with a headdress and wings the color of blood.

I move from painting to painting. There's even one of Will. Shhhh whoosh. Shhhh whoosh. I feel like I'm falling, looking at the paintings, the Weeping Willow singing in my ear, falling into the sounds, and falling into another universe that has a different language.

Shhhh whoosh.

Shhhh whoosh.

Ding.

Shhhh whoosh.

Shhhh whoosh.

Ding.

Someone grabs my arms and spins me around.

"What the hell are you doing?" JAX yells.

I fumble out the earbuds. My mind is buzzing with neon-colored superheroes. She maneuvers her chair and slams the closet doors closed. "You have a huge problem with privacy."

I stammer, "Incredible. I don't...have...words. Why are you hiding them?"

"That's none of your stupid business!" she yells. She looks me up and down and smirks. I'm wearing a new pair of green corduroys and new boots and a black turtleneck. "Oh, the master of secrets is talking to *me* about hiding."

I know we're not talking about her closet paintings anymore. Or just about my clothes.

"I'm sorry. I'm sorry. How many times do I have to say I'm sorry!"

"Why are you here?" she says, going to her art table.

"I told you. I need the forest illustrations."

"Why? The stupid report isn't due for a few weeks!"

"I have a plan. I'm going to send the report to my landlord and see if he'll stop the logging."

"Yeah, that sounds like it'll work," JAX says, rolling her eyes.

"I have to do something!"

"Oh *now*, you're going to *do* something!"

I start crying. "You don't know what it's like...I can't take it anymore, listening to them sawing down the trees. Listening to the grief of the forest."

Her eyes are set against me, and I start hiccupping and stumbling over the words, and all the sadness comes up, like yelling it all at Blue was just the beginning of the layers and layers of *feelings*.

I'm screaming now, spit coming out of my mouth. I'm bent over in the middle of her room, screeching like a saw. "You have no idea to see everything and dream everything..." I'm crying harder now and can't stop..."and not to be able to do anything about it. Ever. And when you try to, everyone blames you for *everything*." I scream the word everything and hyperventilate and sit on the floor.

"Oh gawwwwwwwwwd!" JAX cries, "Cry me a river."

I get up and stagger to the door. Mom was right, what she said to Angel in the shed. This isn't a dreaming gift I have. It's a curse. A life-long curse I'll never ever get rid of.

"Yeah, run away. You're good at that," JAX spits.

I turn. "What do you want from me, JAX?" I'm exhausted. I want to curl up in my bed, and not get out of it for *centuries*.

"You could've stopped the accident!" she yells. "You knew! You knew!"

"I know..." I say, holding the doorknob, defeated. "It's all my fault. I know."

She turns her chair around so her back is to me. "Go on, leave then. You're dismissed."

"Good!" I yell.

"Good!" she yells back as I storm out the door. I want to run to Blue, to sit with Blue, I want it more than anything in the world, but I can't take what they're doing to the others, so I walk the long way back along the road and down the driveway and go inside and lock myself in my room.

An hour later, my phone dings, four times in quick succession. I look, expecting Angel.

It's JAX! And there are images, black ink renditions of the forest. Some of the trees she's drawn are now just stumps. I cry.

"TY! TY! TY!" I text back.

She doesn't reply.

It's 9 in the evening, and I'm in the kitchen. Dirty dishes cover every surface. The floor is filthy. I go into the living room and there is pet hair on the carpet, sofa, curtains. My clothes are piled high in the laundry room. I can't take it anymore.

Then the phone dings. And I think it's JAX again, but it's Aunt Angel this time. "That's it, kid. I'm getting no answers at your house and I'm worried. My sister is on her deathbed here, and I need to know you guys are OK. If I don't hear back tonight, I'm sending in the calvary."

I want to throw my phone across the room. She knows what might happen, even if it's just her friend Constance who comes over. What the consequences might be.

"That's it!" I scream. Apollo barks. Twister runs from the room. I go to my mom's room and throw open her door. "That's it!" I yell again.

I storm outside to the shed. I grab the things I need, empty squirt bottle, liquid paint, a blank canvas.

I dump the canvas beside my mother's bed.

"Maisie...what?" Mom says with a raspy voice. I just see her eyes, lost in the pile of dark covers.

"Enough," I say. I fill the squirt bottle full of paint. I put it in her hand. She won't hold it. I wrap each of her fingers around the bottle one by one.

I tip her hand and squirt a line of the orange paint on the canvas.

"Paint!" I say to her.

She lets the squirt bottle flop sideways, and I straighten it and grab her wrist, and squirt another line of orange.

"Paint!" I scream. "Do it!"

She dribbles dots of orange. I wait, arms crossed. She paints a line, then a circle. She sits up.

I take the paint bottle from her hand. "Message Angel." She grabs for the paint. I hold it away from her like candy. "Do it! Tell her you're OK. We're OK. Keep texting her back or she's going to send someone here and our whole shitty lives are going to get a lot shittier."

She fumbles for her glasses on her nightstand. Types in a message. I feel sorry for her now and want to go get a brush and brush her hair.

But I don't have time. I have an email to write to the landlord.

At the computer, Apollo and Twister plop on top of my feet. They've been all over me since the logging started. Macon goes on and on about how animals talk if you just listen, and I've been looking at Apollo and Twister differently. Like I look at trees. Like there's more there, and I've been taking them for granted.

On the computer, I have Macon's report on Ms. B's visit. I add the alternatives to logging. I put in the alternatives to wood. I go through and insert JAX's illustrations.

I sit back and scroll through. It's beautiful. It's real. It's like a professional photographer came and took a portrait of our woods. Like a family portrait hanging above a mantle.

I go into Mom's room to get the landlord's email. She has the light on now, and she's standing above the canvas. She seems to be painting long lines of trees, an orange forest.

I get the landlord's email from her.

"Thank you," she says, not looking up from her masterpiece. "Thank you."

I go back to the computer and compose an email.

"Dear Mr. O'Brien. I'm doing a report at school on the forest here on your property. I wanted to send some of it to you with illustrations done by JAX Watanabe (neighbor). The research and some of the writing was done by Macon George (neighbor). I thought you might find it interesting.

Did you know there are so many different ways to do logging now, and so many different things people can use instead of wood?

Thank you for reading it.

Sincerely,

Maisie-Grace LaForet

I bite my nails as I hit send. I have too much nervous energy, so I decide to clean the house. I hear Mom in the shower. I vacuum, and when the shower stops, I run water in the sink and do the dishes. I run a load of laundry.

It's late, but I make dinner, boiling water for some ramen noodle cups I find in the back of the cupboard. I put one on Mom's side table, and eat mine. There's still no reply to my email. I give up and hunker on the sofa not really watching a movie. Mom comes out in clean sweats and a T-shirt and joins me. I don't know how long her bout lasted this time. I lost count of the days.

Mom's phone rings. Twister jumps off my lap. Apollo barks. I think it must be Aunt Angel, and say, "Answer it. Tell her we're OK."

"Hello?" Mom says.

"Yes, Ted, she's right here," she says and hands me the phone.

Ted? The landlord? I take the phone nervously. "Hello?" I say.

"Maisie-Grace, I'm calling about your email."

"Yes?"

"My wife and I looked over that report, and we cannot thank you enough. We're going to hang up the art. That'll be OK, right, to print out the pictures and hang them up? As you friend about that, OK? We really loved what Miss Bartholomew had to say about the forest. We had no idea about some of the things she told you."

Great!" I say. I bury my face in Apollo's neck. It's working. It's working. Now he'll stop the logging.

"It's a great eulogy for the forest. That's what Viv, err Mrs. O'Brien says, what a great eulogy. What Miss Bartholomew said was so poetic. I feel that way in the forest, too. And to have pictures to remember the trees by. That was just awful nice of you to prepare this for us."

Eulogy? Isn't that what you say at a funeral? It all sinks in at once. He thinks I'm like a priest giving the forest its last rites.

More is said, but I don't remember. I hang up and throw the phone and it bounces off the couch and hits the floor. I run outside, run down to Blue, pick my way over fallen limbs and a sea of tree trunks, until I'm standing in the middle of the devastation.

"I quit!" I yell, my voice with no trees to stop it traveling to far away hills and echoing back to me. "I quit!"

Later, I'm in bed and Mom crawls in with me.

"I'm not going to school anymore," I say in a flat voice.

Mom sighs.

"I'll go one more day to tell everyone that I quit."

"Oh, Ladybug," she says and squeezes my hand.

BLUE

Chapter 32

When the child brought the others, we asked them to scream their sorrow. Just as we take their carbon dioxide and give them oxygen, we can take their fury and mulch it.

If a tree doesn't get enough light, it grows sideways, seeking the rays. We don't think the sideways tree is bad. We see beauty, the necessity of twisted growth.

We revel in angles.

Humans have lost so much, seeing themselves as bad or wrong for sideways growth. They have forgotten the wisdom of slant and tilt. They have forgotten there are hundreds of ways to grow from a seed, a thousand flowerings, a million ways to find the light.

We see each child as she screams her sorrow. Each has such a different way of seeing. We know there exists a kaleidoscope of possibility in a sea of sight.

The one child, the tall one named Macon, has an animal way, a dirt and stone way. This child thinks this way of seeing makes her wrong or different. She is who she is. She is the seed growing into the fullness of her animal body.

The girl they call JAX is a singular person, a rareness of spirit, a new energy. We feel the brokenness of the body, the hard shell and we see the beauty. Sideways makes her strong. Sideways makes her interesting. Sideways is her journey.

We wish all of the children could hear us.

Your grief is truth.

Your grief is power.

Your grief is beauty.

We grieve. We grieve falling to the machines, of course we do. Of course, we will miss the love of the soil, the touch of the sun, the scampering of paws. Still, in that grief, we understand the transmutation. We understand going from one energy to another, from roots to roof. We can see the purpose in that.

What do we truly grieve? That people do not know us. Refuse to really *know* us.

We grieve the lack of celebration of transition. We grieve the lack of stories told, the loss of legend, the death of mythology. We don't think humans understand this. The emptiness that comes without the stories.

Without the passing of the wisdom.

Chapter 33

I try to tell JAX and Macon in homeroom but I can't get the words out. I try to tell them I'm quitting school, that today is my last day, but it sticks in my throat. Homeroom is over and we scatter to our classes, and I decide to wait until we're all together in Miss Sullivan's class.

In English, I can't stop staring at the poster, "If you see something, say something."

My whole life is seeing stuff without being able to say it.

I'm seeing something and I'm saying something and no one will listen!

Everybody I know sees differently. There's how Angel sees with her cards and incense, how Mom sees with her buckets of paint, how Twister sees as she shoots like lightning through the forest, how Blue sees, her canopy so far up she can see so far. How Macon sees animals. How JAX sees in line, texture, and perspective.

At school, there's a lot of talk about diversity. Diversity in the ways our brains work and diversity in races and genders and sexual orientation.

But what about the different ways of seeing? What about the voices of the animals and the trees? All around us, they're cutting down old forests and planting Christmas trees. Every year, more forests go. Less polyculture and more monoculture and nobody says anything. Why aren't we fighting for earth diversity as much as we're fighting for people diversity?

After English class I go to Mr. Altishin's desk, the "If you see something, say something" poster hanging behind him. I don't know why I'm here. It's the poster. It won't leave me alone.

"Yes, Miss LaForet, how can I assist?" Mr. Altishin doesn't look up. He has a red marker and he's grading papers. His desk is covered in stacks of papers and they fly off the sides of the desk like birds. His hair sticks up. I stare at his untied shoe.

Two weird things happen as I'm standing there. I realize I like Mr. Altishin, really like him. He's weird, and I like that. This surprises me. The second thing is I feel sad because I realize I'll miss him when I quit school. This surprises me more.

"Yes, Miss LaForet?"

I don't know how to start. I think of the doll and the yellow block making the transition from home to school, and how I need a sketch to show me how to talk to people, how to build a bridge so people can understand.

"Mr. Altishin," I whisper, "do you believe people have dreams that come true?"

He looks up, a red line on his cheek where he accidentally tattooed himself with the marker. He leans in and says in a whisper, "Are you talking about the earthquake?"

I shake my head. People act this way all the time since the earthquake, either veering around me because they're scared of me, or whispering "earthquake" to me like it's a haunted secret.

"No. Yes." I say, confused. I don't know what I want from him.

I point to the poster. "What if you see lots of things and you try to say them and nobody will listen?" I'm not planning on telling him what I'm really thinking but it just slips out. I'm building this conversation bridge and don't know if the bridge will fall while I'm talking.

"I guess what I mean is do *other* people *also* dream things that come true? Am I the only one?" I also want to ask him then what to do when nobody will listen or they call you a freak, but I'm too overwhelmed.

He sits for a while, tapping the back end of the pen on the pile of papers. Then he looks up and laughs. He picks up a tattered copy of a paperback from a stack of falling down paperbacks on the other side of his desk.

"Yes!" He holds the book in both hands toward me as if he's making an offering. "Artists and writers see what others cannot see all the time! Many of them dream their books, dream their characters. I believe books are as real as anything else in the world. They're able to write about everything they see and give it to people to read. So, yes, I do believe in dreams; I do believe they can come true. And I do believe there are people out there who shout them from the rooftop even when most people won't listen!"

I look at the browned pages of the book he's holding. I think about my dreams and visions and watch them come alive right there with Mr. Altishin. I watch my visions fly like birds and settle as words on a page. It's a new idea, one I haven't had before, the visions becoming nouns and verbs and adjectives and I'm surprised when tears come into my eyes.

I hear a voice in my heart whisper, "Write down your visions, Maisie-Grace."

Then I remember the loggers and the browned pages of the paperback become the trees I've grown to love. I stumble toward the door.

"Miss LaForet, this book is for you!" Mr. Altishin calls after me.

I keep running.

***

Miss Sullivan's class is next, and I'm nervous about telling JAX and Macon I'm quitting, so I go to the classroom early. I hear Miss Sullivan's raised voice as I approach. She's upset. I sneak a peek. She's talking to the principal. Something isn't right. The principal is saying there's something wrong with the way she's teaching. I've seen the principal sitting in the back of our classroom a few times. Miss Sullivan is the best teacher I know so it doesn't make any sense.

"...number of parents who are complaining. You're in a rural community here. This focus on activism it's just riling things up. Besides that, and you know this, we're required by law to teach the curriculum. The students *must* pass the tests..."

I can't hear what Miss Sullivan is saying, so I sneak another peek. She's standing tall and her shoulders are back and JAX's painting of her flashes so strongly. I swear Miss Sullivan is wearing a cape.

Suddenly her voice is very clear.

"Well, I quit!" she says.

***

Macon comes up chatting nonstop, and we enter the classroom. I'm trying to catch Miss Sullivan's eye but she's staring out the windows. The principal leaves and Macon keeps talking. Miss Sullivan is a tree that's being cut down. I can't get the image to go away.

I guess quitting really fires Miss Sullivan up, because the flames are shooting from her as she turns from the windows starts class. We're working on the Call-to-Action part of the report.

"How will you spark a revolution?" she cries, eyes burning. "How will you change the world?"

Will and his posse start goofing around. She goes up to him, stares intensely down into his eyes.

"You have one chance this lifetime," she says. "The world is falling apart. What will you do?" She makes a fist at her stomach. "What will you do, Will Masterson?"

She turns to the rest of us, looks about to say something but sighs instead, goes to the board, and writes: *"There's a price to pay for speaking the truth. There's a bigger price to pay for living a lie." – Cornell West.*

"What do you think Cornell West is saying here?" she asks.

I yell out before I can stop myself, "If nobody listens to you, it doesn't matter how much truth you tell."

Miss Sullivan stops. She looks at me for a long time. The class is quiet. A kid coughs. Miss Sullivan says, almost as a whisper, "Does that mean we shouldn't even try to speak?"

She doesn't wait for an answer. She turns and writes Activism in large letters, and then marks through half of it and turns the word into Action.

"What action will you take? That's what I want you to decide today. What action will benefit your community? I want practical actions that you personally can take to make a difference."

A girl named Meredith raises her hand. She has the best grades in school. "Can you give us some ideas on the action part? What you're looking for?"

Miss Sullivan shakes her head. "It's not about what I want. It's not about grades. It's what *you* want. What kind of world do *you* want?"

I'm quitting school. That's my action, I want to yell. *I'm getting out of here just like you, Miss Sullivan!*

When we break into groups, Macon and JAX are debating the call to action but I'm not paying attention. I'm waiting for Miss Sullivan to circle around so I can announce to her and everyone that I'm quitting. So, I can show her I'm on her side.

She stays way too long with Will and his boys, but finally, she's coming toward us.

I say to Macon and JAX, loudly so Miss S can hear, "I have an announcement."

"Yay, Maisie-Grace," Macon says, clapping.

I say it just as Miss Sullivan arrives at our desks. "I'm quitting school." I turn around and catch her eye. She knows I know. I can see it. She knows I heard her talking to the principal. "Today is my last day!" I fold my arms.

Macon throws herself across the desk. "No, no, Maisie-Grace, no!"

JAX looks at me, and I see something there, something different, but she turns away quickly. "Whatever," she says.

Miss Sullivan stares at me a long time. "You need to focus on your call to action now, OK?" she says and walks away.

I watch her for the rest of the class. She won't look at me, but when the bell rings, she says, "Miss Laforet, may I have a word?"

"I know you're quitting. I heard it at the door!" I blurt when we're alone. "Mom home-schooled me for years. I'll just go back to that. I'm not quitting education, just school!"

She leans back against her desk and folds her arms. "You're not quitting because I'm quitting?" she asks.

I say in a rush, "No, I decided last night." I tell her about the logging, about our report, about sending a draft to my landlord and what he said. "Nobody cares and nothing makes any difference at all!"

She looks at me steadily. "Maisie-Grace, I've been watching you for weeks now. And I think there's something you're figuring out here at school that I'm not sure you can figure out by being at home."

"I'm quitting," I say again. "It's useless! *You're* quitting!"

Miss Sullivan leans down and looks me in the eye. "To be a warrior you have to know when and where and how to fight, OK? You have your bridge to build, and I have my bridge to build. We're in different places. Do you understand?"

She knows about the bridges!

"What's the point of building a bridge if nobody will let you build it all the way to the other side, and there's no way to cross it?"

She stands up and walks around, looks out the window. "That's actually a really great question." She's quiet for a while and then comes back.

"I think we live in times where we have to build our part of the bridge, even if there isn't another side to attach it to. I think we have to keep building, and hope that someday there will be a way to cross it."

I cross my arms and won't look at her. It sounds impossible and exhausting.

"Why do you get to quit and I don't?"

"Maisie-Grace, I see myself in you." I look at her now. We're alike. My heart beats faster. "I want you to have the tools you need to build that bridge. I'm going on to build a different bridge now. Don't worry, I won't stop building. Just promise me you won't stop."

I set my jaw. *I'm quitting! I'm quitting!*

"Please, just think about it, OK?"

Then the weird vision comes again, I watch her skin turn into bark, and needles grow from her hands, and she becomes a very old, very wise tree.

And somebody is always trying to cut her down.

Chapter 34

I *do* think about it. On the bus ride home as we pass forest after forest being logged. As I say goodbye to Macon and she keeps begging me not to quit school. As I'm walking down the driveway between abandoned Christmas trees.

I think about leaving school, about Miss Sullivan, about the trees I hear every day crashing to the ground.

I think about it all as the sky turns suddenly dark and it starts to rain. I stop to have a conversation with the birches who are losing their leaves. I hear whispers but cannot make out words. I think about the alternatives to wood that nobody seems to care about. I repeat hemp and bamboo and soy and cork until it turns into a song that I sing under my breath.

"Bamboo, soy, and co-ork. Soy, cork, and ba-amboo."

I'm thinking, thinking, thinking. I turn the bend in the driveway and see my mom.

Something's not right. She is talking frantically to one of the loggers. No, it's not a logger, it's the landlord. He keeps backing up and she keeps moving toward him.

Something's wrong with Mom, the way she's standing, the way she's thrusting her face forward. I can feel it in every fiber of my being.

Something is horribly wrong.

I run.

I drop my backpack. My hat flies off. My scarf takes to the wind.

I run.

I run.

As I get closer, I see Mom's holding Blue's scarf ribbon. It's smeared with mud.

"Mom?"

"Oh, Maisie-Grace," she cries. I look to Mr. O'Brien but his face is turned away.

"Mom!" I scream and run full force. Mom grabs at my hand as I pass, but I yank away. I run hard down the logging road, past the machines, falling, crying, getting up, running, running, running. I fall and roll halfway down the hill.

I stop.

The whole world stops. There isn't a sound. No wind. No birds. It's as if everything is holding its breath.

In front of me is a giant stump where Blue used to be.

They chopped down Blue.

They *murdered* her.

Her body is on its side. Her upper branches in the gully.

I stare at the stump. It's a huge flat stage, the color a light tan. So different from the dark mossy wood of her trunk. The smell is sweet, and I feel like I'm going to vomit. Blue's rings are there, hundreds of them.

I fly out of my body and watch myself from above. I want to scream, but I can't speak. I want to touch Blue, but I can't move.

Mom is by my side, sobbing and trying to hug me.

"The logger said he wasn't told anything about Blue," she says. "I called Ted and he came right out. Ted swears he told him. Oh Maisie-Grace, it doesn't make sense. They left her alone before, so why now?"

She's clinging to me, but I'm a zombie. Her voice is far away.

Mr. O'Brien walks up.

"Maisie-Grace, I'm sorry about this. Here," he says. He's upset, too. But I don't care. I don't care about anyone or anything. He takes a checkbook out of his front pocket and writes on it. He tears it off and puts it on Blue's stump. The rectangle of paper is a tiny square on Blue's giant base. I stare at it. $5000. It means nothing.

"I guess I'd better give you your money back," he says to my mom.

They put a price tag on the forest and turn it into a shopping mall.

"No! No!" I want to kill the landlord, but instead, I turn to Mom and hit her with my fists. "No! No! No!" I look at the scarves in her hand at Mr. O'Brien and I'm so full of hate I'm ready to *kill* someone.

I scream, a roar that echoes back through the decimated forest.

I want out. I have to get out of here. I run, hard back up the hill, until I'm back at the house, because where else was there to go for comfort now that Blue is gone?

Where?

MACON

Chapter 35

No no no no no no no...Maisie Grace can't quit school. She can't. She can't. She just can't. I call her but her mom picks up and tells me what happened with Blue, and I feel like someone punched me in the stomach because this is what's going to happen to Jinx.

And Barney and Walnut and Anastasia and Goat.

Next weekend. My dad and brothers do the butchering themselves. Some of our neighbors send the animals away for someone else to do it, then what comes back are cuts of meat wrapped in white paper. We do the killing up close and personal. I hide in my room, but you can still hear it.

That night I'm at dinner and Mom is serving pork, and it's all I can do not to grab the side of the table and turn the whole thing over, spill the food all over the floor. I'm thinking about Maisie Grace quitting, and Blue dying, and my best friends losing their lives. And I'm just so mad and so frustrated and I'm about to burst with it.

And Olaf is leaning against me, and Mom is putting a pork chop on my plate, and I say so loudly Olaf growls, "No, I will not eat a pork chop!"

And my dad yells and yells, and raises his fist, and I close my eyes, and scream, "No! I will not. And I will not eat bacon!"

Because they kill everything, Blue and Barney, and everyone and everything, and someone has to say, No. No. No!

And the boys start shoving me because Dad taught them a long time ago how to be "men", and finally when it's getting really bad, Mom intervenes, and she's never done that before.

"Dad," she says, "Macon is getting older, let's let her make her own decisions." He screams and spits, and screams some more, and she says, "OK, let's let her make this one decision, OK?" She pats his head like he's a dog. "OK? Just this one."

And he says, "Well, I wash my hands of her then," and he's moving his hands around like he's washing them and it's like he's washing the pigs' blood from his hands, and I think, *You should wash your hands. You should.*

And I'm shaking and my brother stabs the pork chop and takes it off my plate and no one says anything else, and I don't have to eat it.

I don't have to eat it!

***

Maisie-Grace doesn't come to school for a few days, and I don't know if she's really quit or if she's mourning Blue, so JAX and I go by her house, and she's in bed in a dark room, and I sit on the floor beside the bed, and I hold her feet. And I think, *Wow would they beat me up if I let myself fall into my feelings like this, what a wild house where you can feel your feelings*, but I don't say anything.

I just hold her feet.

JAX

Chapter 36

Run away! Run away! Oh, MG, you're quitting? Big freakin' surprise.
All you ever do is run away.

A voice inside my head says, "You told her to leave that first time." And I tell the voice to shut up.

I get home from school and get into bed. Dad asks, "Jaja-chan, are you OK?" Because he knows after all those months in bed, I'd never be in bed willingly.

I tell him I'm OK, because there's nothing wrong with me, I'm just perturbed. Yeah, that's the right word – perturbed.

Why is MG leaving perturbing me? I don't know. Who cares, leave.

And then I look up. At the ceiling. And someone is flying across it. Someone I've never seen there before. I cry out:

"Mom?"

"Mom?"

She's on the ceiling. Wearing a cape. And she's flying

I can't stop weeping, my pillow soaked, Dad knocking at the door and me telling him to just go away. Just leave me alone.

I've been willing Mom to show up so I could paint her for years. But she never ever did. It wasn't just that she died. It's that I never saw her again. Anywhere. In my dreams, I saw the crash, but never her, just rolling and broken metal and my broken body. She never showed up on the ceiling and when I tried to draw her from scratch, I couldn't. I just couldn't.

You've come.

You've finally come.

And I appear, too, right next to her, and my cape isn't stuck anymore and we're flying together, over the plaster swirls and into the corners and back again.

I haul myself to my art desk, and the images fly from my hands with furious speed. My phone dings and it's Macon and

I ignore it. It dings and dings and dings, and I turn it off and throw it across the room onto the bed.

When I finish the sketch, I sit back. I feel a peace I haven't felt in years, or maybe even ever.

When I turn my phone back on, it rings immediately.

"What!?" I yell into it.

Macon garbles something I can't understand. Then she says it's slower, but I can't quite believe it. "What?"

"Blue...is...dead," she says, each word distinct like a knife.

I can't think. Blue dead? I can't fit it into my brain. It doesn't seem possible that something so huge and alive could be dead. The feeling reminds me of something, of Mom.

"OK, OK. Look, I have some stuff I have to do first. But meet me at MG's driveway in like two hours," I say.

I have to paint Mom. The rough sketch just won't do. I can't put it off. I feel an urgency I don't understand. Aquamarine and antelope brown and gold for the hair, and me next to her with a crimson cape.

Mom and me.

Flying.

***

MG doesn't even turn around in bed when we come into her room. She's facing the wall, and it's like she's down some dark black hole. All of it is so familiar. The dark room. The bed. The grief. I know this.

Macon holds her feet, and I just look at her outline in the bed and I realize I've been blaming MG for the accident, and how much she carries because she sees so much, and I start crying, and I can't stop.

But then when we leave, I know what I have to do. I know what I have to do for MG, for the forest, for all of us.

I know my call to action.

BLUE

Chapter 37

Her bed is a hole and she is letting herself sink, and fall, and crumble. She is decomposing into the soil, dissolving, disintegrating. We stand at the window and watch. We sink with her.

Don't be afraid of death. It is just a transformation. Can you see?

"Yes, I see, but..." The child says, and stops and thinks for a while. "It's not the death that hurts."

No?

"No, yes, it *is* the death, but it's more. It's the way you all died. Ripping off branches and trees slamming together. Like nobody cares. The loggers didn't get to know you all at all. At all!"

Tell the others, this.

The child cries and we watch her tears.

They have silenced us. Your silence is just more silence. Can you see?

She cannot stop crying.

Come with me, Child.

"I don't want to."

"Come."

The child rises, and we lead her outside in the dark in her bare feet. We stop on the porch because she will need shoes in the sharp desecrated forest. She puts them on. We lead her through the forest of the young, down, down, down, to us. It is a crisp night, the moon half hidden by clouds.

"I don't want to be here!" she cries, and turns to go but we stop her.

We whisper in her ear what we want her to do. It takes her a while to understand what we're asking. But then she gets it. She goes to our stump, falls to her hands and knees and starts digging.

It's a long way down now, through piled branches and chips of bark, layers of a fallen forest. She finds the hole. She dips her hand in. Inside are all of her buried dreams, dreams she called nightmares, but they were more foretellings in a painful world.

She takes them out one by one.

Cone.

Rock.

Stick.

Bark.

She puts them in her pockets, until they bulge to bursting.

She walks our fallen trunk, running her palm over the bark, following our trunk down into the gulley, brush and grass, sometimes taller than she is, and all we can see is her upraised palm moving along our bark. We appear to her as a blue dancing ghost emerging from the fog

"Are you a saint now or an angel?" the child asks.

We're still here. We will always be here.

Many hours later, we send the mother a dream to wake her. She jolts upright, runs to the girl's room to find the child gone. We have shown the mother in the dream where to find her.

With a flashlight, the mother makes her way through the forest of the young, down the widened path, over the debris of the others, to the place where we are resting sideways.

It is not easy to hike into the gulley. She holds our bark as she climbs down, over branches and boulders. She slips and falls and pulls herself up. It is a long journey to the top of our canopy.

There, the child is nestled in the crook of one of our upper branches, face surrounded by stems and bouquets of needles. She is hugging us, and we are hugging her. Her pockets bulge with her unburied dreams.

The mother picks her up. With the moon to see by, she carries the girl out of the gully and up the long hill.

MAISIE-GRACE

Chapter 38

There are needles in my hair. How did they get there? Morning light comes through the curtains and shines on the dresser. On it are sticks, cones, bark, rocks. I remember now what happened the night before. I stare at the objects, each one a dream that came true. Even though they are bad dreams, they're real. They are me. They are mine.

They are ours, I hear Blue say.

"Ours," I say out loud.

I look at my phone. It's almost 9. I see the date, and it seems important, but I can't figure out why. I try to go back to sleep, but something is urging me awake. That date. That date.

Oh, today is the day of the presentation!

I jump from bed and dig frantically in the closet. I forgot I put all my wild clothes in a trash bag and finally find the bag. Flower power dress, green polka dot leggings, boots with frogs on them.

I take a shower. When I come out into the kitchen, Mom drops her mug and it clangs against the table, coffee spilling everywhere.

"Ladybug!" she cries, jumping up and hugging me so hard it hurts. "What do you want? What can I get you? Here, sit. Sit. What are you hungry for? Granola? Let me get you some. I have some blackberries."

"I have to go down to the forest."

"Oh, Ladybug, are you sure? Is that a good idea?"

"I have to, Mom. I have to go talk to the trees. The ones that are left."

I say it before I realize I'm saying it. For the first time since I was little, I've just told my mom I'm talking to the trees. I look at her sideways, scared of her reaction.

"Good, honey. Good," she says. And then she says the craziest thing. "Tell me what they have to say, OK?"

Twister jumps off his perch on the windowsill and follows me as I go to the door. "Oh, and when I come back, can you drive me to school?"

***

Lisa Michaels' and her team are at the front of Miss Sullivan's class as I walk in. The front board is covered in Monarch butterflies, orange wings, and black designs. The orange and black fill my vision.

"Maisie-Grace!" Macon screams, running and lifting me off the floor. She's wearing the jersey dress and the boots, and she looks fantastic.

"You're actually here!" JAX calls over to me.

"Everyone quiet down," Miss Sullivan says. "Maisie-Grace take your seat now. Macon." She points. "Now! Please." I settle in between JAX and Macon. JAX reaches over and puts her hand on my shoulder and keeps it there. I stare at her surprised. She won't look back, but she's smiling. I glance over to Miss Sullivan, and she nods at me.

Lisa goes back to her presentation and her "call to action". I've been thinking about that since this morning when I picked my way through the downed trees. It wasn't just that they were no more, that the humming of forest voices was silenced. It was the way it was done, limbs torn to shreds. Trees cut to aim at other trees to knock them down. It all seemed so violent, so unnecessarily violent.

I've been thinking about my call to action, the forests' call to action. Blue's call to action.

"So, it's actually not hard or anything. We have handouts. You really can raise monarch butterflies in your backyard." Lisa passes out the handouts. Raise butterflies? It seems to me like a dream.

A good dream.

"Now that's activism," Miss Sullivan says and claps.

Will and his buddies go next. They have on Blue Jay jackets and their faces are painted blue and gold. High school football is the community they've chosen. Will's brother is a running back.

Most of Will's research is what his brother told him. One of the guys in the group is writing a bunch of x's and o's on the board with arrows. Will talks about the quarterback, running back, tight ends, the football field, the number of wins last season. The boys keep jumping and butting chests.

Will ends with, "So I guess the call to action is: Don't be a loser. Go see a game."

Miss Sullivan says: "OK, boys, thank you. Have a seat. That was insightful and local, good job. OK, who's next?" She scans the faces and catches my eye. "Maisie-Grace, come on, you're up."

"We've been practicing this, Maisie-Grace," Macon whispers to me as we walk up. "Do you want to just let us do it?"

"OK," I say. "But I want to do the call to action. Is that all right?"

Macon flips through her notes and finds the last page. "OK, here's what we've got."

"No, I don't need it. I know what I want to say."

Macon grabs a half dozen poster boards at the back of class. They're covered so you can't see them. I help her.

Macon does a great job of talking about *our* forest (because it's not my forest anymore, it's ours and it's the first time I see that). About what Miss B told us, the mythology and the science. She describes the different trees and animals. She waits until the end to tell the class that they're logging the forest, and cutting the trees down. She looks at me like she's going to cry and thank goodness she doesn't mention Blue, or I don't know how I'd hold it together.

Macon turns back to the class and says: "We wanted to do an unveiling of the art all at once. For those who don't know, JAX is an amazing artist."

JAX goes from poster board to poster board and flips back the cover paper.

"We have two sets. You could say one set is the science and one is the mythology."

It's like a dream, another *good* dream. Here are the black ink sketches of Douglas Fir trees, giving us cross sections, and tree rings, and roots, and mushrooms, and squirrels—realistic and with the tiniest details, like the ones I saw in her bedroom.

But over here. Over here! The color. The whimsy! She's created a whole world like the one in her closet, of trees and ferns and clouds and dirt pulsing with texture and tint and magic, but it's more than that.

There's one that's bigger than the rest. It draws me forward like a magnet, but not just me, Miss Sullivan, but not just her, everyone in the class, until we're all like a colony of bees buzzing around the queen.

It's Blue, rainbow colored, and muscular. And round her, we're flying—JAX, Macon, and me, with capes.

The painting pulses like it's alive. Pulses like Blue pulses. JAX really "saw" her. JAX fell in love with Blue. I look up and Miss Sullivan is looking with tears in her eyes. And I can see right through her, and I can read her mind. *This is why I teach. This is why.*

"Now for the call to action, it's Maisie-Grace's turn," Macon screams because everyone is roaming and chatting so loud.

"Everyone! Back to your desks. Now," Miss Sullivan says, wiping her eyes with the back of her hand.

I turn. They're all staring at me. I can't move. I can't breathe.

"Maisie-Grace," Macon whispers, motioning with her hand because I can't move. "Go. Go."

I look out at all the faces.

Breathe in.

Breathe out.

Breathe in.

Breathe out.

I feel an energy lift me up. It moves up my ankles, into my spine, bringing me to my tiptoes. The kids in front of me transform into an old growth forest, messy and tumbling over each other, connected with invisible threads. Some are trees and some are ferns and no one is better or worse and we all just need to allow ourselves to *be*.

The energy keeps moving through my body. I am filled with it.

Tree Wisdom.

The words tumble out of my mouth. "Our call to action is that we want everyone to go home and make friends with a tree. Find one tree. You can give her a name. Have a conversation with her. Talk to her every day. Become friends with a tree. But most importantly, you have to listen to it. See if you can hear it talking to you."

"Snowflake!" Will laughs. He high-fives his buddy in the next desk, misses, and falls face first out of his desk. Everybody laughs.

I take another breath. I'm not finished. There's something else.

"But not just a tree, OK? You can pick a wild animal." I look at Macon. "Or a farm animal. You can pick any plant. Or the river. Give them a name. Listen to them."

I stop now, and look over the faces of the other kids.

Breathe in.

Breathe out.

"There's one more thing. I want to tell you about my friendship with a tree named Blue." I go over to the painting. "What I want to tell you is about how I spoke to Blue…"

"And she spoke back."

I have my notebook, old and covered in dirt, the notebook I used to write down Blue's message so long ago.

I open it and start reading.

JAX

Chapter 39

Black is perfect for a funeral. No wait, "ritual" – that's what MG called it. I put on the black jeans and black dress shirt, but something just doesn't feel right. But for the first time since I was a kid, I realize with genuine surprise, I don't want to wear black.

I find a pink T-shirt at the bottom of a drawer, a sheer flowered blouse that belonged to my mom, pink skirt, and fishnet leggings. I open the closet. It's no longer a hidden gallery. I have my whimsical art all over the walls of my room now. I can be proud to be goth and I can be proud to be whimsical. And if anyone has a problem with that, well they can suck dirt.

At the bottom of the closet is a gift my Dad bought for my last birthday that I've never worn. I take them out of the box — blue cowboy boots with embossed yellow flowers.

I put on pink glittery eye shadow, pink blush, and neon pink lipstick. My fingernails are already pink. I stare at myself in the full-length mirror and laugh.

What do they call this? "Pastel goth?"

Pastel JAX.

I look at the time on my phone and realize I have just enough time. I go to the art table and write quickly, switching out and using different colored markers.

MG asked us to write a story about Blue to share at a ritual. Some sentences are in Prussian Blue. Some red. A paragraph is in purple. One section I write in black but make all the verbs green.

My real story about Blue is the painting – my way of telling a story is through art. There's a lot I don't write. I don't write about how Blue's death reminds me of my mom's, how I cried for Blue as if the tree actually *was* my mom, how the two deaths seemed to blend into one.

I don't write about how I tried to hide the crying from Dad and failed, how we sat and talked, and how he said, "I have wanted to speak about your mom with you for many months, *musume*."

How we sat up way past midnight and laughed and cried and told stories.

I finish the Blue story, fold it, and put it into my pack. I check the time. I still have half an hour.

There is something else I've been thinking about doing. I take out a clean sheet of art paper. Beside the paper are a dozen art pens lined up, the colors of the rainbow.

I pick up a blue pen first.

"This is a story about my mom," I write.

MACON

Chapter 40

Olaf and I arrive and it's like a graveyard, a forest graveyard, so many tree stumps and they look like old hunched people who've fallen over from exhaustion.

Maisie is in a shimmering blue dress with a blue scarf and she's so beautiful with all the brown destruction around her. JAX is already there and Olaf runs and jumps on Apollo and scares Maisie-Grace's cat who jumps and runs away.

Everything is so quiet. Branches and twigs and bark thrown around. I stop at Blue's stump. The loggers must've dragged her body out already.

Then I notice JAX. Is she wearing pink!!?

Maisie-Grace says, "OK, let's get started," and she has a huge carpet bag covered in flowers and yanks things from it— candle, fabric, crystals, incense. She just keeps pulling stuff out.

I play with the folded loose-leaf paper in my pocket, the story about Blue.

Maisie-Grace clears a spot beside Blue's stump and spreads purple fabric and puts down the crystals and candle and incense, and she goes around and picks up fir cones and branches with needles and small stones and I help her and we put them on the fabric too. The candle is in a glass jar and she lights it and the flame flicks around in the breeze.

She holds up something and lights it. "This is a sage stick," she says, moving it around as the smoke billows on the wind. It smells tangy and earthy. "Aunt Angel uses it to cleanse people, so I'm going to cleanse you guys."

When it's my turn, I close my eyes tight and put out my arms like someone is using a wand on me at the airport. The sage smell makes me want to sit in the dirt but I force myself to stand.

Maisie-Grace tells us to get in a half circle around Blue's stump and asks who wants to go first to read their story, and I take out my paper and hold it in my fist.

"I'll go first," JAX says.

She takes out a paper with multicolored writing. She reads about how she kept trying to paint herself as a superhero, but her cape was always stuck, about how one day she woke up and saw herself flying like a superhero over Blue.

"I have to give Blue credit. I think she was the one who got my cape unstuck," JAX says, and wipes her nose. And then she tells us about her Mom showing up on the ceiling, and she talks about painting her mom and she's full on crying now, and JAX does not cry, and she's got the painting with her and we look at it, and she says she knows what it feels like to lose someone you love.

We're all quiet for a while, and the forest is so empty and dead, that it makes me uncomfortable, so I say, "I'll go," and unfold my paper before anyone can say anything.

"The first time I met Blue, I didn't know her name. I was in the back 40 looking for Johnny, our goat. I saw Maisie-Grace over on the other side of the barbed wire fence. I hid so she couldn't see me. We weren't friends then."

I glance up to see if they're listening. They're watching me and I blush and look back down at the paper.

"I saw her spinning and dancing and talking to the tree. She was wearing a red scarf and it spun around with her. It was like a fairy tale."

I clear my throat.

"I didn't know then, but I was about to make two of the best people friends I've ever had, and it's all because of a tree named Blue."

I fold the paper and put it away.

It had been sprinkling all morning and it starts to rain, not a light rain either. We put up our hoods. The altar is soaked, the candle and sage go out, but none of us move.

Maisie-Grace takes out a sheet of paper. The rain drenches it, and the words bleed. She crumples it.

She looks over to where Blue used to be. She goes to the stump, slipping on roots, and climbs up until she stands on Blue's rings.

She spreads her arm. I can't tell if it's rain on her cheeks or if she's crying.

She spins around, and she spins faster and faster in her blue dress and scarf, rain soaking her to the skin, and OH, how scared I am she'll fall.

We wait, but she never says any words. She just spins and spins and spins.

MAISIE-GRACE

Chapter 41

Four months. Five. Six. It's not like it's over. I guess I thought Blue would be the end of it, but they still have to log the rest of the forest. The searing buzz of saws. Whoosh, boom. Whoosh, boom.

Whoosh.

Boom.

The soundtrack of my life. I go back to school because I can't take it, my body can't handle the vibrations. But it's more than that. I'm still figuring out how to build the bridge and bring the others back. Whatever that means.

Logging trucks piled with logs stir up dust as they crawl down the gravel driveway. Mom stays out of her dark place, just my dark place is like a yo-yo. Some days I'm good. Some days I'm horrible.

Blue's spirit is here. But it's the physical I miss, the crumbling bark, the sappy smell, the slickness of roots in the rain. Just because I can feel their spirit, doesn't mean my whole body doesn't miss their body.

I don't go near the forest now.

***

Eight months later on my 12th birthday, it seems to be over. The logging trucks are gone. The forest is gone. It's a Saturday.

I'm on the sofa. I'm thinking about turning 12, and I'm just not sure of the benefits of growing up in this world.

Angel shows up. I don't get off the sofa.

"Come on, kid!" she puts out her hand. Hesitantly, I take it. She pulls me off the sofa. "We've got something to show you."

They drag me toward the back door. I put boots over my footy PJs. They drag me all the way through the yard to the shed. I know it's my birthday. I know they probably have gifts for me. What do I have to celebrate?

"Happy birthday, Ladybug!" Mom yells, throwing open the rotting shed door.

Propped on an easel at the doorway is a massive canvas, JAX's painting of Blue, but it's even more alive now. The painting magnetizes me forward. It moves and writhes, so thick with paint the texture is like bark—layers and layers of color and texture. So many layers that you'd see one tree, then another would emerge. And another. And the three of us flying,

I run my finger along a ridge of bark paint, and further up to the thin sharp pine needles. As I touch the painting, I feel my body or my soul or both growing. I grow until I'm bursting through the shed rough, until I'm as large as Blue.

"JAX spent a lot more time on it," Mom says. "She wants you to have it. You can put Blue up anywhere in the house, OK?"

I nod. I don't know what's happening. I want to curl up in the painting.

"Kid! Sit!" Angel says, pointing to my corner table. "We got some celebrating to do. Twelve is a big deal. Twelve is the beginning of so much."

Mom and Angel gather gifts and a covered cake stand and bring them to my table.

Mom takes the lid off the cake. Inside is a tall chocolate cake. "Macon and her mom made you a vegan birthday cake. Can you believe it?"

"Macon's mom made a vegan cake!?" I ask.

"You know I may have been wrong about Mrs. George," Mom says as I stick my finger into the icing. "JAX and Macon are coming over later for dinner. Let's save it for then, OK?"

She hands me a box with a big bow. She painted the wrapping paper with some kind of reflective paint and I can see my face in it. I open it. Inside is a thick handmade journal. I take it out of the box. The paper has twigs in it. It's thick and rough and uneven. The cover is the same as the painting of Blue on the easel.

Mom says, "No trees were hurting in the making of this journal."

I turn it over in my hands.

"I took recycled paper and leaves and twigs and turned it into pulp. I asked JAX and Macon to give me their stories of Blue, and I printed them on recycled paper and mulched them, and included their words in the pulp. And I sprinkled every page with essential oils, vetiver, and frankincense. I watched a video to learn how to do the binding. And I had Angel do a blessing on it."

It's rough in my hands, like some natural thing you'd find growing in the woods. I put it to my nose, and it smells like roots plunging into soil.

Mom glances at Angel and kneels beside me. "Sorry, Maisie," she says. "I'm really sorry. I was a jerk about your dreams. And you don't deserve a mom who's depressed."

She hands me a marker. "This is for your dreams, Maisie-Grace. I want you to write them down. My gift is art, and your gift is your way of seeing, your dreams, your predictions, how you can hear what the trees are trying to tell us. And I'm sorry I didn't see that before."

I stare into her green eyes, her blonde hair pulled back. I get up from my chair and search the studio until I find it, stacked with her art books in the corner. "1001 Tips and Tricks." I carry the heavy book over.

"This is for you," I say. I hand her the book. I don't say, *You need to figure the depression out. I can't keep doing this.*

She won't look me in the eyes, but she holds the book up against her, and I know she gets the message.

Angel says. "Kid, you've got another gift to open," and plops a big heavy present in my lap, wrapped in purple paper with silver stars and moons. I tear off the paper. Inside is the dusty red book of magic she brought to our bootcamp that first day, "The Alchemy of the Sacred".

I open the book randomly, and it's full of herbs and spells and incantations. "More tips and tricks?" I ask.

"Oh, it's much bigger than that." She puts her hand on my shoulder. "I'm passing this book down to you. Treat it as sacred. You're gonna to need it. We're all going to need it."

BLUE

Chapter 42

They come from the south, the west, the north. It's our anniversary, one full revolution of the earth around the sun.

Olaf and Macon run through fields, parting wild grass as they make their way. JAX pumps her chair down the empty road, over the rocky driveway through the weedy path. Through the forest of the young trees, Maisie-Grace, Apollo, and Twister tumble downward.

The three meet at the place where we used to stand. Here and there a few saplings still grow.

The child stops at one of the saplings. "Hello little one," she says, holding the needled branch. The sapling is taller than the child. "My name is Maisie-Grace. If it's OK with you, I'd like to get to know you."

The sapling, taken by surprise, whispers something, words like a song, and the child perks her ears.

The child bends and whispers. "I'll be back,"

"Ready?" Macon asks.

The three girls follow the path, down through our devastation. It's foggy, and there are hundreds of tree stumps as far as the eyes can see. Brush and blackberry vines twist up and cling, turning the logging road into a path again. The girls stop to pull vines and limbs back so they can pass. They move down the hill into what used to be the middle of the forest. Now there is light and sky where before there was canopy and coolness and shade.

They don't speak. They keep their heads forward and their purpose clear.

We have a surprise waiting for them.

They round a bend. They stop, staring, mouths open. The forest floor is bursting with a sea of wild daisies. Thousands – tens of thousands – of white and yellow blooms blanket the forest floor, covering the field, hugging the tree stumps, peeking up through vines. They grow in clumps as tall as the girls.

A message for the girls. A sign that things do grow back. That joy can return.

They laugh and throw themselves into the blooms, heads popping up like blossoms. Maisie-Grace twirls. JAX draws. Macon lays on her back, dogs tumbling over her.

Each pick a messy bouquet carried in their fists.

They continue their journey. Deeper they go, farther and farther. They leave the logged forest behind. The path disappears, the shrubs and weeds grow thicker. They must stop and clear more of it to get through.

Beyond the old growth forest, another forest is hidden. The child does not know of it until now. It isn't so thick, nor so tall, nor so old. It's not old growth, but newer trees of many different forms.

Thorns pull at their clothes. They help JAX through the ruts. They yank tree branches out of the way.

There are more trees here with leaves and fewer with needles. Each turn in the path is a different ecosystem, another miracle, a "good dream".

They come to a group of alders that cling to a creek. We urge the child toward them. She feels drawn, like they are her family, their thin white mottled bodies, the lime green grass below, like they are her ancestors.

Alders, we whisper. *Elders.*

Alders.

Elders.

"What about here?" the child asks, picking her way into the middle of the stand.

"Yay!" Macon says.

"Perfect," JAX says.

They put down a blanket.

Macon carries JAX and puts her down.

From their packs, they bring out food.

Maisie-Grace lifts out her journal. It is still blank. We know she's been unable to write her dreams. Unable to mark up something so beautiful.

JAX withdraws a sketch pad.

Macon has a book on animals.

They each lean against an elder, JAX reaching out a hand to the bark. The dogs curl together. The cat perches on a mossy log.

The child turns to the Alder behind her. "I'll have to figure out a name for you. Give me time. It'll come to me."

She opens the journal. The handmade pages are like bark. She takes up her pen.

"We're listening," she says. Each child is quiet, each listening, each breathing. The others around them, root and bark, are breathing too, listening too.

The girl writes a first sentence.

The ink soaks into the paper like rain into soil. She feels she's inscribing her soul upon the skin of a tree. She feels her roots go down and her arms spread out like branches.

She writes a second sentence.

A third.

As she writes, she's being written upon. The elders are inscribing their wisdom into her, tattooing truth into her neck, her forearms, her cheek-bones.

We, Blue, emerge from the fog for a second, an azure ghost, and the girl looks up and gasps. We hover in the mist, leaning forward, protecting all the girls with sacred branches, wind humming our ancestor's song.

We watch as the child writes, as she weaves visions into stories...

And stories into forests.

About the Author

Caroline Allen works out of a yurt nestled in the woods in rural Oregon, writing novels, creating art, and coaching others. She lives with her goofy Lab/Husky mix, Atlas, and her wise and very old black cat, Pearl. Earlier in her life, Caroline was a newsroom journalist in Tokyo and London, when a sudden spiritual opening led her (kicking and screaming) down the path to becoming a mystic. She is the author of the award-winning Elemental Journey series, four literary novels that fictionalize her journey around the world in search of purpose.

Previous Titles by Caroline Allen

The Elemental Journey series (adult literary fiction) follows a mystic around the world as she comes to terms with her gift in a world rocked by climate change.

***

Earth
ISBN: 0997582405
Winner of the 2015 Independent Publishers' Gold Medal
for Best Midwest Fiction.

In rural Missouri in the 1970s, thirteen-year-old Pearl Swinton has just had her first mystical vision. There is no place for Pearl's "gift" in the bloody reality of subsistence farming and rural poverty. As her visions unfold, she must find her way in a family and a community that react with fear and violence. When Pearl discovers that her Aunt Nadine has a similar gift, she bicycles across the state to find her. That trip unexpectedly throws Pearl into a journey to save her runaway sister and sends her into a deep exploration of herself, her visions, and her visceral relationship to the earth. Told with fierce lyricism, *Earth* is a story about the importance of finding one's own truth and sense of self in dire circumstances and against the odds. It is also a story about the link between understanding ourselves and our relationship with the earth. In this first of the five-book *Elemental Journey Series* that will follow Pearl across continents and into adulthood, Caroline Allen introduces a form of storytelling that is unflinching in its honesty, filled with compassion, and underscored with originality.

***

Air
ISBN: 0997582421
Winner of the Independent Publishers' 2016 Silver Medal
for Visionary Fiction.

Turbulence opens this second book in the *Elemental Journey Series* as Pearl Swinton, now in her twenties, uproots from the Midwest and flies to Tokyo, where she has no job, no friends, and no home, a place where she hopes to live floating above the culture. How will she survive with her mystical visions in a country so foreign from everything she knows? Pearl lands at a Jesuit mission and is magnetized to the ethereal missionary Usui. After she is forced to leave, she is thrown unprepared into the complicated world of Japanese culture and must learn to maneuver friendships, understand love, and balance the intensity of working at one of the city's largest newspapers. When she stumbles upon Usui living as a homeless man, a journey begins that draws Pearl deep into Japan's hidden homeless underworld. Having given up any connection to civilization to "find himself," Usui brings Pearl face to face with her own homelessness and challenges her to begin the painful journey of understanding her visions and finding herself. In the end, hope flies on the paper wings of thousands of origami cranes. Pearl is called to her own mysticism, not just for herself, but for a world where the loss of magic may well be the real threat. A fundamentally radical work of art, *Air* tackles core issues facing individuals coming of age in today's world. How can anyone feel safe and at home on a planet threatened by escalating violence and devastating climate change? Where, truly, is home?

***

Fire
ISBN: 0997582448
Winner of the 2018 Independent Publishers' gold medal
for Visionary Fiction.

Twenty-something Pearl Swinton is on walkabout for a year across Southeast Asia with her boyfriend, Finn. Pearl is a travel writer and encounters a host of dynamic characters, from a boat boy in the Philippines, to a penitent in Nepal, to a rickshaw driver in India, each challenging her world view. In search of her life purpose, Pearl is being pulled more deeply away from all that is familiar on this journey, a path that began when she moved to Tokyo from the U.S. years earlier. Who is the self behind cultural conditioning? Who is she when no one is telling her who to be? What is her calling? The couple ends up in London, where Pearl finds some semblance of home, while Finn struggles to belong in a place he left behind years before. Pearl ultimately realizes that before she can go upward and understand this illusory "purpose", she must journey down into the self and heal. In the end, she is faced with a decision that could reduce to ashes the life she has built, and destroy all that she holds dear.

***

Water
ISBN: 0997582464
Winner of the 2020 Independent Publishers' Gold Medal
for Visionary Fiction.

Water opens with Pearl Swinton drowning in a dark night of the soul. In the depths, she hears a cry to purpose, but to what? A former journalist who has spent years trying to outrun her psychic visions, Pearl meets a mentor in an urban mystic named Rayne, who introduces her to the concept of the Divine Feminine and sets her afloat on the turbulent waters of self-acceptance. Pearl finds herself navigating Seattle's metaphysical scene, studying tarot, shamanism, and past-life regression. As a journalist, she gave voice to the voiceless, and in the transformative journey she's now on, she is being asked to find her own voice. Accepting her new mystical calling finds her at the helm of a rickety folding table in the back of a bookstore reading tarot for the public. Daily she dives deep into the psyches of many, finding inside each person a lushness and a rootlessness, a poetry and a thirst. Still Pearl resists this life. Still she runs away. It will take a national tragedy to break through the walls of her resistance and show Pearl how desperately the world needs her to step into her power, to own the divinity of the feminine voice.

From the Author: Thank you for purchasing *Blue*. It's my dearest hope that you got as much joy and wisdom from reading it as I did from writing it. I learned so much writing this book, and I hope you did, too. If you have a few moments, please add your review of *Blue* to your favorite online bookseller site. If you'd like to connect with me and learn more about my past and future books, or if you'd like to hear more about my writing and mystical coaching, please visit my websites for news, recent blog posts, and more. Remember to sign up for my newsletter: CarolineAllen.com and CarolineAllencoach.com. And please don't forget to talk to your favorite tree. They're listening. Sincerely, Caroline Allen

OUR STREET
BOOKS

JUVENILE FICTION, NON-FICTION, PARENTING

Our Street Books are for children of all ages, delivering a potent
mix of fantastic, rip-roaring adventure and fantasy stories to
excite the imagination; spiritual fiction to help the mind and the
heart; humorous stories to make the funny bone grow;
historical tales to evolve interest; and all manner of subjects that
stretch imagination, grab attention, inform, inspire and keep
the pages turning. Our subjects include Non-fiction and Fiction,
Fantasy and Science Fiction, Religious, Spiritual, Historical,
Adventure, Social Issues, Humour, Folk Tales and more.
If you have enjoyed this book, why not tell other readers by
posting a review on your preferred book site.

Recent bestsellers from Our Street Books are:

Relax Kids: Aladdin's Magic Carpet
Marneta Viegas
Let Snow White, the Wizard of Oz and other fairytale
characters show you and your child how to meditate and relax.
Meditations for young children aged 5 and up.
Paperback: 978-1-78279-869-9 Hardcover: 978-1-90381-666-0

Wonderful Earth
An interactive book for hours of fun learning
Mick Inkpen, Nick Butterworth
An interactive Creation story: Lift the flap,
turn the wheel, look in the mirror, and more.
Hardcover: 978-1-84694-314-0

Boring Bible: Super Son Series 1
Andy Robb
Find out about angels, sin and the Super Son of God.
Paperback: 978-1-84694-386-7

Jonah and the Last Great Dragon
Legend of the Heart Eaters
M.E. Holley
When legendary creatures invade our world,
only dragon-fire can destroy them; and
Jonah alone can control the Great Dragon.
Paperback: 978-1-78099-541-0 ebook: 978-1-78099-542-7

Little Prayers Series: Classic Children's Prayers
Alan and Linda Parry
Traditional prayers told by your child's favourite creatures.
Hardcover: 978-1-84694-449-9

Magnificent Me, Magnificent You – The Grand Canyon
Dawattie Basdeo, Angela Cutler
A treasure-filled story of discovery with a range of
inspiring fun exercises, activities, songs and games
for children aged 6 to 11.
Paperback: 978-1-78279-819-4

Q is for Question
An ABC of Philosophy
Tiffany Poirier
An illustrated non-fiction philosophy book to help
children aged 8 to 11 discover, debate and articulate
thought-provoking, open-ended questions about
existence, free will and happiness.
Hardcover: 978-1-84694-183-2

Relax Kids: How to be Happy
52 positive activities for children
Marneta Viegas
Fun activities to bring the family together.
Paperback: 978-1-78279-162-1

Rise of the Shadow Stealers
The Firebird Chronicles
Daniel Ingram-Brown
Memories are going missing. Can Fletcher and
Scoop unearth their own lost history and save the
Storyteller's treasure from the shadows?
Paperback: 978-1-78099-694-3 ebook: 978-1-78099-693-6

Readers of ebooks can buy or view any of these bestsellers by clicking on the live link in the title. Most titles are published in paperback and as an ebook. Paperbacks are available in traditional bookshops. Both print and ebook formats are available online.

Find more titles and sign up to our readers' newsletter at
www.collectiveinkbooks.com/children-and-young-adult